Escape to Mars

By Andrew Tristem

For Rebecca, Toby and Rose

Table of Contents

Prologue

As the star faded, the delicate gravitational balance between its planets began to destabilise. The two biggest started to duel for supremacy, until one was flung out of the solar system, to begin a ten-million-year journey across interstellar space.

***

Jack sat down at his desk and looked at the results again. He felt sick to the pit of his stomach. He'd run the simulation three times and checked all the inputs again and again.

Jack, a junior scientist with the European Cosmos Observatory, was working late, to track hundreds of rogue planets detected by the organisation's new space telescope. Thousands had been found darting across the Milky Way, since it was launched three years earlier.

He reached for his phone and rang his manager.

"Martin, I think I've made a major discovery. You need to hear this," he said.

Martin sat up in bed and switched a nightlight on. His wife was dozing next to him.

"It better be pretty important to wake me up at 1am," he whispered.

***

When news broke that a wandering planet from a far-off solar system would collide with Earth in just over 79 years' time, the world didn't panic as some had imagined. After all, 79 years was longer than most of us expected to live. Of course, there was much anger and protest. But people kept working, and the world economy continued to grow, albeit slowly from that time on.

Disaster movies quickly emerged, always with happy endings. But as the days and weeks passed, and we started to understand the physics, we realised that any attempt to nudge the planet off course would be futile. It was just too big. We only had one chance - to find a new home in the stars.

The United Nations announced an ambitious plan to relocate one million people to Mars by the time of the collision. A global lottery would give passage to hundreds of people every month. It gave us the hope we needed. Hope for humanity. Hope that we might escape the cataclysm.

And so, we started to build a fleet of spaceships that would be sent from Europe, America, Asia, Africa and Oceania to our new home.

Chapter 1: Mission to Mars

"Lift off, on humanity's latest trek to the red planet,' said Bernie, the moustached television commentator, as the array of 36 rockets fired in unison, blasting chunks of debris hundreds of feet into the air. The Spaceship Resolute lifted its massive cargo of people and supplies from the ground, as it headed on the long trip to Mars.

"The tenth of ten thousand ships offering hope to all humanity," added the journeyman presenter, as the 200-metre rocket pulled clear of the launch pad. It had been stationed at Cape Canaveral for two weeks while its cargo of materials needed for the colony were loaded on board.

The crew were professional astronauts from the Space Corps rather than lottery winners. But it was the prospect of winning a ticket that was really firing the public's imagination. Hundreds were undergoing training in the deserts of Utah. And the first of them would be flying to the colony in less than a year's time, once the basic infrastructure was set up.

"Twelve more astronauts to add to more than 100 already on their way," said Bernie, his red face lighting up one corner of the screen as the rocket powered into the atmosphere. "Operation Hope is in progress, and the people of Earth are watching with pride," he said.

With 69 years left before Collision Day, a rocket would fire every few weeks, increasing to every day, to take people to the city being built on the red planet.

A lottery was about to be held on television. I had my ticket, hopeful that fortune would favour me. Not everyone felt that way. Many people preferred to live out their lives on Earth, accepting the end as inevitable, rather than endure the extreme conditions expected on Mars. I was under no illusions but still dreamed about playing my part.

"Escape velocity has been reached. The rocket will continue to the rendezvous point, where the crew will hold up for two days while the ship is refuelled, before flying on to Mars," Bernie continued.

I pulled out my wallet and discreetly checked my ticket was safely inside.

I had long wondered how I would cope with leaving Earth if I won a place. To see the blue planet fade into the distance as the ship sailed away.

Chapter 2: Lottery

"I'll give them two years at most before they're all dead," said Tom, gesturing dismissively at the screen, before sipping his beer.

The rocket was almost out of sight, just a small dot on the television screen, as the jet planes filming it were left in its wake.

"That's if they survive touch down," he scoffed.

He had a point. All ten ships were on course to the red planet, and landing would be one of the trickiest bits. The spaceship had never been tested on Mars. So, if one crashed, they all might. But that was the kind of risk that had to be taken, given the time frame.

"If they don't make it, the next batch will," I said, trying my best not to get riled.

Tom, a friend I'd met at my first newspaper job, swivelled in his seat to look at me.

"You can't think any of this makes sense, George?" he said. "It's just a way of keeping the masses quiet until the big crash."

He'd become a bit of a conspiracy theorist since the rogue planet was detected.

He was not part of the growing cult that denied the collision was coming, though. Those people were widely ridiculed on television.

"It's the only hope we have," I said suppressing some irritation. "I'd prefer to do this than just give up."

I hadn't mentioned that I'd bought a lottery ticket - I couldn't bear to have a conversation about it. It would quickly turn into a heated argument with neither of us likely to back down. Our friendship was already teetering on the brink because of our diverging views. Mine positive, accepting the course of action. His, believing it was all a waste of money that was ruining the years he had left. It was true that the world was gearing up to spend 20 percent of gross domestic product in the effort, sucking money out of businesses and taxing people to the limit.

The television switched to adverts and one for the lottery came up.

"Be like one of the pioneers of the Wild West, and join our voyage to the new frontier," said the narrator in a calm, baritone voice, as we watched pictures of a rocket blasting from Earth.

"Those old timers faced the same struggle as humankind is today – to build a home in a hostile faraway place," the narrator continued.

Then a lottery ticket filled the screen with the slogan, 'Will it be you?'

"Will it be you to travel to a planet with no atmosphere or soil, where you will probably starve to death," said Tom.

I sighed in resignation, then watched the winning numbers flash up one by one on the screen – "2,4,2,19,25,24,17,14,12."

"Poor fools," said Tom slurping his drink. "I'll enjoy it here on Earth until the very last moment."

I discreetly checked my ticket against the numbers – "2,4,2,19,25,24,17,14,12."

Chapter 3: New job

The mental high I felt for the first two days after winning my ticket is difficult to convey. It was akin to someone who'd fallen out of a plane and somehow survived by landing on a gigantic feather bed. That thrilling feeling of escapism enveloped me everywhere I went. But gradually my endorphin levels dropped to normal, and I got down to the business of settling my affairs before the start of training.

As an orphan, my parents having died in a car crash when I was just two years old, I had no next of kin to break the news to. My stepmother had thrown me out aged 14 after an argument about a tattoo. Going into a children's home after years with a family felt like a final kick in the teeth. But in some ways, I was lucky. A vicar who worked there helped me pass my exams so I could get an office job, and I decided to move from my rural home in southern England to London and train as a reporter.

My difficult upbringing made me a more empathetic person. I would go out of my way to help someone. And I spent years building a close circle of friends.

Telling them I was leaving was one of the hardest things I'd ever done. Harder than surviving in a home. I was single, though, so other than my friends, I had little to keep me on Earth. Or that's how I looked at it at the time.

***

"Congratulations on winning a ticket to Mars," said the Human Resources officer at the plush lottery headquarters in St James' Square, London. "Please make yourself comfortable, and I'll talk you through what happens next."

I took a sip of the coffee he'd made, while he looked at my CV.

"We try to give everyone a job that matches their skills. Something you'll do in addition to all the routine work on Mars," he said. "You're the first journalist to go, so we've set you up with a news outlet."

"Brilliant, which one?" I asked.

"We've linked up with World News One," he said. "They're really first rate; we've worked with them for many years. If you're happy, I'll set up a meeting with their news editor?"

"I'd be delighted," I said.

Less than an hour later, I was driven to their offices near Tower Hill underground station, to meet news editor Martin Shivers. On first sight, the offices were less impressive than I expected. The giant blue building they were housed in looked more like a shopping mall than home to the world's premier news organisation. Inside, though, it was a different matter. At the foot of the escalators leading to the newsroom, stood a 1960s printing press as a nod to a bygone era. At the top of the steps was a statue of the owner, a tall Swedish billionaire who'd cornered the market in British media. It gave me a feeling of awe to be in the same building.

I buzzed the door and one of the hacks directed me to Martin, who was working on a story.

"Welcome dear boy to our humble establishment," he said in a mildly clipped accent. His enthusiasm for life undimmed by 30 years in newspapers. "So, you're going to write lots of lovely Mars stories for us, I hear?"

He took me into his office, a dingy space off the main newsroom, and asked who I'd worked for.

"Most recently, the Hampstead Press," I said. "I ran one of the editions for two years. My first job was at the Somerset Sentinel though."

"Both excellent papers," he said. "We'll want lots of colour pieces from you. Every cough and spit of what goes on during the trip, and after you get there."

Chapter 4: Training

Commander Jane Davey oversaw the training programme. She behaved more like an army drill sergeant than an officer from the prestigious Space Corps. You might have expected her to be sympathetic to the lottery winners, but nothing could be further from the truth. She only wanted the Space Corps personnel to go and resented the rest of us for taking up precious places.

The commander seemed to target me from the beginning. The first day I got there, she marched down the line and stopped when she got to me.

"Exactly what's your skill, Hodges?" she said reading the name tag pinned to my chest. "What are you going to bring to the Mars party?"

"I'm a reporter," I said. "It'll be my job to write about the journey, and life after we get there."

"You might think we need scientists to help us grow food, or engineers to build shelters. But we've got reporters," she said dismissively.

She took a couple of steps back so everyone could see her clearly.

"The Space Corps will need to turn you 'Lots' into useful members of society or the mission will fail," she said.

It was the first time I'd heard us described as 'Lots.' It wasn't a pleasant term, but it was something we'd have to get used to.

Training lasted three months if you passed. Those who failed had to repeat it until they did.

One day, Commander Davey turned up when we were training to meet one of the physical fitness standards – 40 slow push-ups in two minutes for men, 20 for women.

"None of you are in shape," she shouted, her blonde hair tucked neatly into her cap, as she strode down the line. "You're going to be here for the rest of your lives."

She believed only the most capable people should be chosen for the colony. The best technicians, architects and medics. In short, the Space Corps.

I tried to keep in good spirits, remembering why I was there. I made no wisecracks. Once we were on Mars though, all bets were off.

The programme was designed to prepare us both physically and mentally for what lay ahead. Every two days, we did pull-ups and press ups. I improved just a little each time until I reached the standard. But after the first six weeks of training, I was still unable to complete the obstacle course in the allotted time.

It was then that I met Sally. She had sailed through all the tests and encouraged me to keep trying.

"If you train twice a day, your times will improve rapidly," she said. I took her advice and went for an additional two-mile run each evening. After a few days, my times suddenly improved, and I comfortably met the standard.

"Congratulations, you've done it," she said at dinnertime. I probably wouldn't have passed without her.

Mental training was even harder for me. It focussed on what they called 'isolation preparedness,' which was, in fact, a test of how we would cope living cheek by jowl 24 hours a day. Four of us were locked up in extreme close quarters for six weeks with no means of communicating with the outside world.

The only way I survived the claustrophobia was to read the great books of my youth: Three Men in a Boat, Catcher in the Rye, One Flew over the Cuckoo's Nest, to name a few. I read them over and over to escape the mental turmoil created by caging us into 20 square metres of accommodation. More gave up during isolation training than anything else. Those books helped me scrape through.

"You've done better than I imagined," said Commander Davey after I came out. "I had you down as someone who'd bolt. The mind can do funny things to you in there."

Another mental test came when we recorded goodbyes to our family and friends. Several candidates pulled out of the programme after seeing their parents in tears. It was a cruel test. You had to be genuine, no joking around. I prepared myself and said my piece to my closest friends while shedding a tear. It didn't change my mind though.

When graduation day came along, only a few out of every 10 had passed.

There was a swift handshake from Commander Davey, as she called out the names of those who'd won their places.

But, as I left the building to go to my quarters, she beckoned me over. "You're flying with me," she grinned.

Chapter 5: Blast off

The clock ticked down to sixty seconds before take-off. Twelve of us were strapped to our seats, nervously watching the seconds disappear, knowing we were facing the most dangerous part of the journey.

I found myself visualising a catastrophic explosion, then reflecting that the odds were on my side. The risk of disaster was put at three percent. Quite low, but high enough to give you butterflies.

I settled down with the thought that nothing could be done, our destiny was already set.

Final checks were carried out by computers with seconds to go, so the flight could be stopped at the last moment if anything was spotted.

"Five, four, three, two, one. Ignition."

The rockets roared into life and the starship began to shake like a cheap fairground ride. Our arms and legs were pushed hard into the padded seats, as 3G of gravity kicked in. I wriggled my right leg, which was pinned uncomfortably.

As we began to gain altitude, the rocket rolled on its back and accelerated again. The noise was almost unbearable, despite my headset and the ship's sound insulation. After a minute or so, we went supersonic, which put maximum stress on the ship. I closed my eyes and prayed it would hold together. The first stage separated, and the second stage ignited. "So far so good," I thought. I glanced at the rest of the crew - they were all in their own worlds, praying everything would be okay.

The second stage cut out and a third and final one ignited, taking us serenely into space. After a couple of minutes, the rockets stopped burning and gravity subsided to zero. In just eight minutes we'd gone from ground to space. But all I could think about was the intense nausea I was feeling. It felt like I was continuously falling, as my stomach floated inside my abdomen. I looked through a cabin window to get my bearings and saw Earth looming beneath us. It was the last time I'd see her so close.

"Rendezvous at the living quarters in five minutes for post take off checks," came the order through our earpieces. I unstrapped myself and inched along to a set of steps, which led to the quarters.

"How did you find it?" I asked one of the Lots called Sandy.

"I'll tell you tomorrow after I've had time to recover," she said.

Once we'd gathered, Commander Davey gave us our first set of orders. "Your job is to send a report," she told me. I'd prepared it in advance, so it only needed a few tweaks before I could mail it to my editors on Earth:

"Blasting off from Earth blows your mind to another world

Nothing prepares you for blast off - the excitement, anticipation and adrenaline is unlike anything I've ever experienced. Physically, the rocket pushed me to the limit – but the mental challenges were my biggest battle..."

The living quarters were designed to produce a small amount of artificial gravity. The section of rocket containing them could whirl around 10 times every minute, creating a centrifugal force of roughly one twentieth of Earth's gravity. The rate of spin was slow enough to avoid dizziness once we got used to it. But it would produce enough force to prevent the most debilitating effects of long-term exposure to zero gravity. To put it another way, it would keep our bone and muscle tissue just strong enough for the Mars landing. At 38 percent of Earth's gravity, touching down on the red planet would be a big shock to the system.

The living quarters were kitted out differently from the rest of the ship, with the furnishings laid along the inner circumference of the rocket because the centrifugal force pushed us towards its walls. We were soon toddling along the curves of our new home, as it whirled around.

"Now for the next stage of the trip," said Commander Davey after we'd finished our tasks. "Get ready for the ride to Lagrange 1."

Lagrange 1, a point of gravitational equilibrium between the Earth and the Sun, was the site of an enormous fuel depot. Our ship would refuel there before setting off on the eight-month journey to Mars. Sandy prepared dinner and called us to the table. Like me she was aged 21. All the lottery winners were young because it was only open to people aged 21 to 35. Those older would die before the collision anyway, and those younger would get their chance as the years ticked by.

Politicians had recently decreed that people shouldn't have children within 70 years of the collision date. Anything less would be unfair to those coming after us. Most of us agreed but it meant that the Space Programme would run out of young people well before the collision.

"You'll have to get used to this food," Commander Davey told us as she chewed on a piece of grey processed meat. "And it's not going to get any better on Mars."

It didn't look great but tasted okay. I tucked into mine without complaining.

"The engineers have confirmed that everything has gone smoothly," the commander continued. "So, we can start our journey."

Lagrange 1 is roughly five times the distance from Earth to the Moon, and it took us three weeks to get there.

A team of six astronauts operated the depot, which contained a dozen giant fuel tanks. They guided our ship alongside one of them, connected a nozzle and pumped fuel in. It took six hours to fill our tanks.

"You might as well take a long last look at Earth," said Commander Davey once the operation was complete. "It's going to disappear pretty quickly once we set sail." I could already cover it with a thumb on an outstretched hand.

The engines blasted early the next morning, and we felt the ship accelerate to cruising speed. Earth was rapidly shrinking into a little blue dot behind us.

"You will have prepared yourselves mentally for the journey ahead," said Jill, our 'health and wellbeing' officer. "But there is nothing like the real thing. Remember, I am here to talk, should you have any issues."

I had no intention of speaking to her about my state of mind, but leaving Earth was giving me nightmares. I'd lay awake in the early hours of the morning, thinking of all the great places I'd visited, and how I would never see them again. I'd dream about the beaches I'd enjoyed in southern England, Australia and Thailand. Then the sand would start to drain away from under my feet, like I was in a giant egg timer, until I was dragged into the vortex along with my surfboard. I'd wake drenched in sweat, but thought it best to block it out. It was comforting to know that there was a listening ear should I need it, though.

To make things worse, the atmosphere on board started to sour a couple of days into the journey. Commander Davey began to make snide remarks about members of the crew when they were out of earshot. She also made great claims about herself, which couldn't possibly all be true. She was a chess champion, a scratch golfer, a sub three-hour marathon runner. Whatever you did, she could do it better.

"At least we won't get bored, listening to all those stories," said Sandy after breakfast one morning.

"Maybe not, but she's supposed to be setting an example," I said. "And you know that if she says things about others when they are not around, she will be doing the same about you too."

I could see she was a leader despite her faults. She had a certain glib charm, and some of the crew hung onto her every word. Others could see straight through her though.

"I set up a business before I decided on a career with the Space Corps," she told us over dinner about half-way through the trek.

"We'd designed a quantum computer at university and needed some funds to develop it. The British banks were rubbish, but the Americans were falling over themselves to work with us. Just shows why it's such a great country. Anyway, we got some amazing results. We got it to a point where the computer could break any encryption anywhere in the world. They were amazed. That's when the US Government contacted me and offered a deal I couldn't refuse."

"What was that?" asked Jill eagerly.

"More money than you can imagine," the commander said. "That's how I got the apartment in New York. But I told them it wasn't about the money. I demanded US citizenship and a place on the Space Programme as part of the deal."

"That's amazing," I said. "I suppose we've never heard of it because it's secret?"

"You guessed it," she said grinning widely. "But I don't suppose it matters now I'm going to Mars."

"How did the computer work?" asked Jill.

"It's all far too theoretical to go into," said the commander. "I got a PhD out of it, but you won't see it in the library. It's Top Secret."

With three months to go before touch down, she dropped another bombshell. "You might as well know, I'm being earmarked to be Mars leader," she told us as we gathered for our daily meeting. "I've been elected to the Mars Council, and the word on the street is it's just the first step." I wasn't sure whether to believe her, although it seemed plausible given her rank.

A few weeks before landing, the commander was complaining to me about the untidiness of the crew. It was the usual type of rant, picking faults in everyone's characters, except the person she was talking to. To change subject, I mentioned that one of my articles had been well received on Earth.

"I suppose I should be wary of talking to you," she said. "One thing I will say is the Space Corps is doing a brilliant job. Tell that to your readers."

I was stunned by her lack of news sense, thinking that such a story would be of interest to anyone. But I just smiled and said nothing.

"We must be realistic, though, life won't be anything like that lottery advert," she continued. "The situation is totally different on Mars. The pioneers of the Wild West didn't need a biodome to grow food, for starters. We'll need to look way back in history for our inspiration. The way we lived thousands of years before."

She seemed to be talking about an age when people scraped a meagre living from the land.

"Surely, we can do better than that?" I asked.

"We can try, but it's the economic reality," she said.

Of all her stories, this was the most newsworthy. It had a clear news line and readers had the right to know what she was thinking. I sent a story to Martin that evening:

Space Corps officer slams 'unrealistic' lottery marketing

Commander Davey of the Space Corps has blasted the lottery advert for Mars, saying that conditions will be far harder than those depicted.

While cruising to the red planet with lottery winners, she said the colony will need to look much further back in history than the Wild West for inspiration.

"Mars won't be anything like the lottery advert," she said. "The situation is totally different. The pioneers of the Wild West didn't need a biodome to grow their food.

"We'll need to look way back in history for our inspiration. The way we lived thousands of years before that. It's the economic reality..."

When the story didn't appear on news channels the next day, I winged a message to Martin asking whether they were going to publish.

"It's a really interesting bit of tittle tattle, but it's not really a runner," he said. "It's not worth damaging your relationship with the commander over this. Send us some more of your colour pieces about the toilets etcetera, that sort of thing."

I was surprised, but didn't take it to heart. He had far more experience than me, and I trusted his judgement.

The remaining days passed without major incident. My reports were a great hit on Earth. They loved reading about the risks of vomiting or sneezing in space, and how we coped when the toilets broke. Being sick, without capturing it, was just about the biggest faux pas you could make. The crew would have to get down on their hands and knees to track down every particle, or the ship would stink for weeks. A close second was failing to catch a sneeze - we all carried tissues to capture the spray, which would otherwise fly on relentlessly into anything in its path. And we were hugely relieved to have a technician on board who could fix the toilets when the suction ducts broke. The consequences of travelling for months without working lavatories didn't bear thinking about.

But the best tales continued to come from the commander. I wondered if she was suffering from a mental health condition, and whether there was even a name for it. A few of us started to call her a bullshitter but that hardly seemed to do it justice. The routine of writing news reports and my other duties, such as helping to clean the ship, meant that I was generally kept busy.

When I was not, I spent time lounging about in the living quarters, which we called the doughnut because of the way they bulged out around the rocket, chatting to Jill, Sandy and the rest of the crew.

Or if I wanted to get away from everyone, I'd seek out one of the ship's many nooks and crannies. I often snuck to the stores to hide away and read a book for an hour. Days turned into weeks, and weeks into months, until finally, we faced landing day.

Chapter 6: New arrivals

"Hold onto your hats, we're going down," yelled Commander Davey as the touch down sequence started.

The ship belly flopped into the thin atmosphere and began to shudder as the heat-resistant tiles buffeted against the Martian air. Sparks flew up from the undercarriage for a couple of minutes until the ship swivelled into a vertical position, and its four entry rockets blasted towards the surface.

Massive g-forces pinned our arms and legs to the padded seats, as we quickly decelerated to a snail's pace. The ship then hovered over the ground for a few moments and gently touched down next to the array of rockets that had preceded us.

"Touch down sequence completed successfully," said Commander Davey joyfully.

I sat still for a moment, getting used to the gravity, which was weighing heavily on my arms, then reached out to shake the hands of the Lots sitting either side of me.

"We made it," I said to Sandy, as we clasped our hands together clumsily.

"Now begins the hard work," she said.

She was right, we were expected to pull our weight on Mars, working in the agricultural dome and taking on other tasks vital to the functioning of the colony. Commander Davey led us through the ship's exit, and we clambered down a short set of steps to the ground below.

The Badwater impact crater, where the colony was homed, stretched more than a dozen kilometres in all directions. Its jagged rim was clearly visible in the thin atmosphere. Beyond it, I could see the gentle slopes of the much larger Hellas impact basin stretching hundreds of kilometres in the distance. A dust devil twisted over some rocks about a mile away.

"This is every bit as awesome as I imagined," I said to Sandy, as we took our first shaky steps on the surface.

"It's breathtaking to see the colony with my own eyes," she said.

A bus pulled up, we heaved ourselves on board, and it whisked us to the Disembarkation Zone. The building was square with a pitched roof and looked a bit like a marquee on Earth.

As we approached, I could see 'Welcome to Mars,' etched on a hillside a few hundred metres away. And 'Passport Control' had been playfully painted on a panel above the air lock at the entrance to the building.

Inside, we were greeted by a stocky Space Corps officer who was sitting at a desk, tapping away at his computer. "Welcome citizens of Mars," he said with a big smile as we approached him. He was dressed head to toe in a UV protection suit. Only his face and hands were uncovered. A bushy beard cut exposure even further. We took off our helmets and sat on some chairs set out in front of his desk, while he took our details.

A few minutes later, an electric bus pulled up behind him, and its doors swished open. "It will take you to your dorms," he said, waving us through.

A network of polytunnels linked the Disembarkation Zone to the colony's main domes. The bus whizzed along, taking us on a winding journey, and stopped outside the entrance to one of them.

"Enjoy your new home," the driver said as we got off. "The concierge will be waiting for you inside."

"Goodbye," I said to Commander Davey. But the door closed before she could reply, and the bus whisked her away.

We walked a few steps along a connecting side tunnel into the large dome, where the concierge was standing with a medic.

"We'll get you checked out here, then I'll show you to your dorms where you'll get a debriefing," she said.

The medic took our blood pressure and checked we were able to stand and walk unaided. The main test was to see if we could stand up three times from a seated position. It was a bit of a struggle, but I was just about able to do it. Once we got the 'all clear,' the concierge walked us a few metres along a corridor, which followed the perimeter of the dome, to Perseverance Dorm 1.

The dorm was separated from the rest of the dome with ten feet high PVC wall panelling. There were no windows on the walls, but natural light flooded in from the clear dome panelling above us. The room was kitted out with a dozen beds, each with a wardrobe and side table. A set of white linen was neatly placed on each bunk.

We sat on our beds, waiting for the debriefing.

Chapter 7: Welcome

"Hi, I'm Alan, your new arrival's helper," said a balding Space Corps officer after arriving a few minutes later. "How was the trip?"

"Too long," I said. "But we made it."

"We've got a great list of things to help you settle into your new home," he said, as he handed out rucksacks of goodies.

"Rehab lasts a week, then you'll start some light duties," he added.

I opened the pack and read some minutes from the latest Mars Council meeting. I could see the commander was on the Board. It was like a town council on Earth, handling things like leisure and cleaning the domes. Earth oversaw all strategic decisions though.

"It's exciting times for the colony," said Jack. "The Council wants us to become more self-sufficient. Agricultural output is its number one priority. It's all in the handouts."

A week gave us plenty of time to digest what was going on. I was eager to type up a story, though, while the day's events were fresh in my mind:

A postcard from Mars

It's 200 million miles away, but Mars feels like Earth's twin to a new arrival - its deserts reminiscent of the arid centre of Australia or the Badlands of the USA. If we could ever terraform this planet, it would be a home from home for the people of Earth.

The colony is being built in the lowest part of Mars, where the surface pressure is the greatest. But it is still less than two percent of Earth's and desperately cold, except for a few short summer months.

Without a pressure suit, a human would die an agonising, blood boiling, death outside the domes in a few minutes. And the risk of ripping our suits is a constant worry. We carry emergency repair packs, essentially large sticking plasters, just in case our suits are compromised.

The relatively thicker atmosphere does, however, cut out some of the deadly UV rays searing through the atmosphere. And growing a beard can help cut down UV exposure as we discovered when we got to the Disembarkation Zone...

There were three main domes in the colony. One was home to 500 Space Corps astronauts. It stood twelve metres high and thirty across. A crisscross of living quarters and work areas lay inside.

The second was home to us Lots. It had a similar design but with side shoots in place to build replica domes as the colony increased in size.

And the third dome, the biggest, stretching some 40 metres in width, was the greenhouse for growing food, known as 'the farm.' All three were connected by a network of polytunnels.

"There are now equal numbers of Space Corps and Lots," I said to Sandy after reading the Council's Colony Dashboard one morning. "But the farm is producing just 13 percent of the food needed."

"I can't see how we can ever feed ourselves," said Tony, one of the old hands who worked with us. "The crops just aren't growing as well as we expected in low gravity. And there's a major problem with mould. An outbreak can wipe out a harvest overnight."

With plans for nine hundred more agricultural domes, to feed a million hungry mouths, the problem was only going to get worse.

Chapter 8: New world order

My muscles grew back rapidly over the first few weeks, as my body adjusted to Mars' gravity. I reached the point where I felt as strong as I had been on Earth. At 180 centimetres and 75 kgs on the home planet, I was always on the slim side. On Mars, I weighed just 28.5 kgs because of the lower gravity. But I could carry lumps of rock that would break my back on Earth. And I could run and jump like an Olympian.

Rice was grown in stacks of hydroponic trays using a water-based solution, which provided all the nutrients the plants needed. To get the water, a group of Lots would trek to a glacier two kilometres away and mine water ice. It was transported back by dumper trucks. The ice was then melted, distilled and all the goodies added. The water was fed into a reservoir, which linked to the irrigation system. We tried not to waste a drop because of the labour needed to get it.

Morale was high during the first few months, as we worked in teams on the farm. But everything changed when, without warning, we were ordered to 'temporarily' increase our hours from eight to twelve a day.

The Space Corps said the extra duty was needed to add more hydroponic trays to the farm, so we could increase production. It meant they would be stacked nearly to the ceiling.

"Let's just refuse to do it," I said to the others. "What can they do if we all down tools?"

But the Space Corps threatened to reduce rations for those who wouldn't play ball. "If you don't pull your weight, then you can't expect the same food," said Jack.

The rest of the Lots trudged off to work, but I refused.

"You don't want to get a name as a troublemaker," said Jack. "You'll be sent to the cells if you're not careful."

With no one backing me, I followed the others.

"This is on Council's orders," said Sandy. "One of the guards told me."

"They don't have the authority to do it," I said. "Stuff like this is supposed to come from Earth."

I hatched a plan to end their scheme. I sent a story to Martin blasting the idea, and the faceless Mars Council behind it.

When it wasn't published the next day, I sent a message demanding to know why. But it was met with radio silence.

A couple of days later, Commander Davey came to see me. "There's been some changes in your role," she said. "You'll need to clear your reports through me from now on. It's come from Mission Control. Sorry."

"But why?" I asked. "That's not how newspapers work."

"Don't worry, I'll just scan over things to check we're all happy," she said. "You'll barely notice a difference."

After that, I had no contact with Martin. I sent messages but heard nothing back. All my reports were sent to Earth by the commander. So I wrote uncontroversial science pieces about growing food on Mars or how to keep safe from radiation.

We planted a new batch of seeds and watched as they grew to maturity.

But, just as Tony had warned us, they bolted to twice the normal height, making them spindly and unproductive. Our gang arrived at the farm one morning, when the crops were just a couple of weeks from harvest, to find a sticky black mould coating them.

"They're ruined," said Tony. "We'll have to rip them out and decontaminate the whole farm." It took weeks.

In response, our working pattern was changed again. We had to inspect each tray for mould on a three-hour cycle. If it was spotted, the trays were removed and bleached. We had to work 14 hours a day to do it. The colony was a step closer to self-sufficiency, but us Lots were seething.

And that wasn't the end of our problems at the farm. There weren't supposed to be any pests on Mars, but some snuck in with the seeds. A plague of spider mites damaged the crops. We blasted them with pesticides, but many plants turned yellow and died. The Space Corps blamed us for the outbreak and demanded better harvests.

"Every calorie counts," was the Space Corps motto.

But the truth was supplies from Earth continued to be essential.

We formed a secret union, swearing and oath of allegiance. We would play along with the system until we got an opportunity to fight back.

"Our day will come," was ours.

Chapter 9: Ice gang

"Step by tiny step, they are turning us into slaves," said Sally who had been rostered to work with me on the farm. "Like heating up a frog in a pan of cold water, they hope we won't notice as the temperature rises, just quietly go along with it until we die a horrible bloody death."

We were speaking in the canteen before tending to the crops.

"If Earth knew what they were up to, they would probably cancel the programme," she added. "Or at least send some bloody troopers."

"The Space Corps are bloody minded enough to carry on regardless, just work us even harder," I told her.

"They wouldn't want a platoon of paratroopers turning up with guns and bombs," she said. "They would take that threat seriously."

She had become our de facto leader, arranging secret meetings, setting the agenda, handing out actions. We could still move freely about our dome, so she organised meetings under the guise of other events.

A card game, for example. If an officer approached, the cards would be quickly picked up to make it look like we were playing.

Like many Lots, Sally had no immediate family. She was an only child, and her parents had died of natural causes a few years earlier.

On Earth, she was a maths teacher at private schools, and regularly rubbed shoulders with the rich and famous. But she had no pretentions. She was resolute and down to earth.

Sally was tall, with long, curly, auburn hair. Her eyes were as big as saucers. Too big, she said, because they needed drops to stop them drying out.

A fork dropped to the ground as we spoke, a sure signal that a guard was approaching. We stopped talking until he was out of earshot.

"We'll get our chance," Sally continued. "Our numbers are increasing every week while the Space Corps' are static. In six months, we could just overpower them. But we need to choose our moment carefully."

Each batch of rice was seeded, watered and harvested on an eight-week cycle. Artificial light was beamed onto the crops to boost production, but the yields remained meagre.

The efficiency drive had only improved production by a few percentage points. So even working us 24 hours a day wouldn't achieve the Space Corps' dream of self-sufficiency. I'd have loved to be a fly on the wall at Council meetings while they discussed their floundering targets.

Every two weeks our work was rotated to mining water ice. And the next day we strapped on our space suits and jumped on the transporter to the mine. Here we worked in freedom to bring back our ration of ice in the permitted time. If we failed, though, we were docked food or given extra duties.

Sally gave me the thumbs up after our final safety checks, and we leaped out of the transporter and onto the Martian surface. A cloud of dust puffed up from our boots as we landed.

The sun was rising above the horizon, casting long shadows off the rim of the Badwater Crater.

Chunks of ice were scattered like boulders around our feet. We started to chuck them into a trailer coupled to the transporter. Occasionally, the two of us would tackle a larger block. They were up to a metre long, but relatively light in the low gravity. We could just about heave them on together.

Sally pointed to something silhouetted in the distance. "It looks like a sinkhole," she said.

It was about a kilometre away, which gave us just enough time to take a quick look.

"That could make it the lowest point on Mars," I said. "We'll have to name it Sally's Sink."

When we arrived, we got on our knees and looked over the crumbling edge. The sinkhole was pitch black below a few hundred feet. "It could be miles to the floor," I said. "Let's sneak back tomorrow with some instruments and take a closer look."

Chapter 10: A new hope

"It's five hundred and twenty metres to the bottom," said Sally after aiming a sensor at the centre of the sinkhole.

"Congratulations, that's one for the record books," I said, peering into the abyss and wondering what secrets it held.

She swiped the gadget to get some more data. "H_2O – water," she said in amazement.

"You've found liquid water down there?" I said, trying to take it in.

People had long believed liquid water could be found on Mars, the only question was how far down you'd need to drill towards the hot core.

"This could change everything," said Sally after taking some more readings. "I'm picking up water in all directions. It's like a lake, George, at least a hundred metres wide."

"How hot is it down there?" I asked.

"It's 15 centigrade," she said, turning to me in delight. It was summer on Mars, but the surface temperature was well below zero.

"That's perfect for growing food," I said. "There must be a heat source."

"This could be the breakthrough we needed," said Sally. "Something to latch onto."

"It's a great find, but I'm not sure how it helps us?" I said.

"Don't worry, I have a plan. Let's speak to John Townsend."

John was that rare thing on Mars, a top scientist who was also a Lot. He could have joined the Space Corps, but he won the lottery, so he packed his bags with the rest of us.

Tall, charming, and articulate, he was a natural leader. He was also Sally's go-to person for scientific advice. He even had the ear of the Space Corps. With a PhD in Metallurgy, they would seek his advice on the best materials to use for buildings. But he still had to work our long shifts and bunked with the rest of us. I tried to learn from him because he was so popular. He had the knack of getting on with everyone. I noticed that whenever he met someone new, he'd ask them lots of questions about themselves, and hung onto their every word.

"It's truly amazing," he said to Sally after she shared the results.

"I'm guessing this is briny water, heated by a fissure of magma below the surface. That's not so surprising since it's in a sinkhole nearly 9km below Mars' surface level."

"Can we use it for the colony, though?" asked Sally.

"In theory, we could stick a dome on top," he said. "Then we could suck in oxygen and nitrogen from the Martian atmosphere, until the air is breathable. If we could use water from the lake to grow crops, the whole colony could move down there. It fits with the colony's plan to use resources as we find them."

"It's bound to be really salty though," I said trying to inject some realism into the conversation.

"We can set up a desalination plant," said John. "We already use that technology for water on the farm."

"This is our chance to offer the Space Corps a deal," said Sally. "We'll build a new dome over the sinkhole if they give us equal representation on the Mars Council. Otherwise, we down tools."

Two guards walked into the dorm at that moment, and frog marched us to the prison cell. We waited an hour before they returned.

"You two," said one of them, pointing at Sally and John. "Come with us." I stood up as they left. "You'll get your turn," the guard said, pushing me back. A full day passed before I heard the march of feet again. I was taken to an office in the Space Corps dome. The door opened, and I stepped inside.

Chapter 11: The offer

"It's lovely to see you again, George," said Commander Davey, holding out a hand.

"I wish it was under different circumstances," I said, shaking it briefly.

She offered me a glass of wine. Something usually reserved for Space Corps officers. I gulped it down a little too eagerly.

"I see you have been busy," she said, grinning widely. "And it seems congratulations are in order."

"But you threw us in the cells," I said.

"That was about a different matter," she said, still beaming. "It's of no consequence right now. Let's discuss your discovery."

"The sinkhole," I said. "It's full of liquid water."

"We've sent a team down, there's a lake," said the commander. "It could make us self-sufficient in a year, if we all work together. There's a shoreline big enough to build an entire town. It means we could have that society you wanted, George. There'll be enough resources for everyone."

"But you need our help?" I asked sceptically.

"Yes, and we need you to disband the union."

"Now I see," I said. "That's why we were arrested."

***

It felt like my face was burning under the bright studio lights, as I stood in front of the television cameras. Beads of sweat dripped down the back of my shirt, the palms of my hands were greasy. We were moments away from broadcasting live to the people of Earth. I tried not to think of the size of the audience, but it would be billions.

"5,4,3,2,1, 'live.'"

"We welcome you from planet Mars with news of a major breakthrough," I said, speaking directly to the camera and trying to maintain a good posture. "A lake of liquid water has been discovered. Initial assessments suggest it could allow the colony to become self-sufficient for food within a year.

"The lake was found at the bottom of a sinkhole, which was spotted by a team mining water ice," I continued. "Lottery winner Sally Weatherall saw it two days ago silhouetted in the sun. She used a laser spectrometer to detect the lake of briny liquid water at the bottom. Further exploration by the Space Corps has confirmed it is more than 100 metres wide, with a shoreline stretching all the way around."

"Thank you, George," said Commander Davey as the camera cut to her.

"Work has already started to turn the sinkhole into our new base. It will give us plenty of space to grow crops and house the colony for the next few years. I can't begin to explain how big this moment is for the people of Mars. While it is only a start, it's exactly the type of breakthrough we were praying for."

"George is being modest, though," she continued, turning to me. "He discovered the sinkhole along with Miss Weatherall. What was that moment like, George?"

I tried to get the words out, but couldn't play along any longer.

"This is all such a sham," I said. "The truth is the Space Corps has been working the lottery winners like slaves for several months. We work fourteen hours a day, six days a week and anyone who complains is sent to the cells. Help us people of Earth, you're our only hope...."

The television screen went bright green as the broadcast was shut down.

Chapter 12: Mission control

"It's a disaster," said the Head of Public Relations for Colonising Mars, as he tugged nervously on his short beard. "Unless we get on top of the news cycle, the story could spin out of control and threaten the whole space programme. God help us, we might be too late already."

"I think you overestimate the risks," said the Minister for Colonising Mars. "It's a bad day at the office, that's all. It doesn't threaten the programme in any way. The polls consistently show we have unshakable public support."

The World Government, which was set up by the United Nations in the years after the rogue planet was discovered, was holding an emergency session to debate the broadcast. It had responsibility for the space programme and global security, while nation states continued to run most other branches of government.

"Virtually all news channels have been running the story since it broke this morning," said the public relations lead. "Some major influencers are calling for the programme to be scrapped - and no one is pushing back. We must counter by the end of the day."

"We can launch a task force within a week to take back the planet," interjected the Head of Starforce Command, a branch of global military invited to the meeting.

"What is the point in having a Starforce if you don't use it when it's needed," he added. "I can put a plan together in two days."

"Agreed," said the World President. "The colony belongs to humanity not the Space Corps. Put your plan together, general, and we'll issue a press release saying we're considering the best course of action. Once we see the proposals, we can say more."

"But Madam President, we need something stronger," insisted the public relations lead. But it was too late.

Chapter 13: Delayed transmission

"Your plan failed at the very first hurdle," mocked Commander Davey. "We edited the broadcast before it was sent to Earth. You don't think we'd be so naïve as to transmit live, do you?"

She was speaking in the canteen in front of hundreds of Lots who'd been hastily gathered after the news bulletin. They were watching silently as the commander ridiculed my efforts to get help. I felt pretty stupid.

"I want to make it very clear to everyone, that Earth is fully behind the Space Corps leadership," she said. "They approve all our plans, so let's put this stunt behind us and redouble our efforts to build the colony."

"She's lying," whispered Sally, who was standing next to me.

"How can you tell?" I asked. "It makes perfect sense. There's a fourteen-minute delay to Earth. Why not just record the show and send it afterwards in case there are any mishaps?"

"They are just not that bright," said Sally. "And why else would they allow you to go unpunished. They must need you for some reason."

"A leopard doesn't change its spots, I suppose," I said. "If the transmission made it to Earth, then they might want me to do another one at some stage."

"Makes perfect sense," said Sally. "Let's just play along for now. If we're right, then we have several cards to play."

That night I dreamt that Earth was coming to our rescue, but their spaceship blew up as it attempted to touch down. Its outer canopy catching fire like the airship Hindenburg, the craft disintegrating as it dropped slowly to the floor.

I woke with a jolt as the camp siren rang out announcing the start of the day. The guards barked orders at us, and we began our first day of work at the sinkhole, digging into the Mars rock with sledgehammers and metal pikes, to lay the foundations. Over the next few weeks, slowly, but surely, our future home began to take shape. Great calluses formed on our hands from the hard labour. I kept looking to the sky hoping that a spaceship was on its way.

Chapter 14: Task Force

"Unrest amid claims the Space Corps is working the lottery winners like slaves," announced Sandra, the red-haired breakfast television presenter on Channel Nineteen. "We have the latest pictures from cities around the world," she added, as a video of burned-out cars flashed on the screen.

Sandra was wearing a lace dress after being advised to sass up her outfits by a Public Relations consultant. She loved fashion, but was wary of the reaction her legion of fans would have for every outfit. Men could get away with wearing the same suits days on end, while female presenters were slammed for the smallest mishap. Showing too much leg would get an immediate negative reaction on networking sites.

She peered at the autocue remembering to sit up straight, her legs neatly positioned to one side.

"We speak to a leading anti-poverty advocate about what the world should do next," she said.

The story had remained the number one news item for several days after the initial broadcast.

Commentators from across the political spectrum catastrophised about developments.

The World Government press release had done little to restore calm. In the void, riots broke out. In just a few spots at first. Then dozens of cities around the world erupted into flames, as police fought pitched battles with anti-colony protesters.

Tom was watching Sandra present the news at a branch meeting of the People Against Poverty Party. It was a London-based political group with just a few hundred members.

"Surely now they'll cancel the space programme and feed the starving," he said to the members, who were sitting around a table at the Red Lion in Chiswick, London.

"Right on, brother," said its leader Bazz Tompkin. "Let's hit the government where it hurts – call for a general strike."

"We need action," said Tom, throwing up his hands in despair. "We need to strike while the iron's hot – march on Downing Street and refuse to leave until they agree to our demands."

"We need to engage rather than enrage," said Tomkins. "Let's register our disgust with a high value press release calling for a general strike unless the programme is scrapped."

"That's pointless," said Tom. "Only direct action will stop the spaceships."

"Why don't you just join the bloody anarchists if you feel like that?" said Tomkins.

***

The ashen face of the World President flickered onto television sets around the planet. The hastily arranged news broadcast was about to begin. Aged 43, the president had risen through the political ranks promising to make a success of the space programme, which was already running well behind schedule.

She was sitting, cross armed, behind a walnut desk, wearing a pastel blue suit as recommended by her public relations advisor. The suit was fitted to show off her narrow waste, one of her best features, according to the advisor. Another was her perfectly symmetrical face. She cut her hair short to show it off, and stop her hair curling too much.

"As many of you will know, news outlets have been running a story about the Space Corps' treatment of the lottery winners," she said earnestly. "I am also deeply troubled by this development.

"We have, therefore, initiated negotiations with the Mars leadership, so we can restore democracy to the red planet. We are confident common sense will prevail but, if not, a task force will be sent to restore order."

She paused a moment for dramatic effect, a trick learned at media training school. "The transport of people will be stopped until this situation is resolved, although provisions will continue to be shipped," she said. "While the discovery of a water filled sinkhole gives us great hope for the programme, we cannot allow the reckless actions of the Space Corps to risk what I still believe is mankind's greatest ever achievement. Four heavily armed ships are therefore being prepared for the long trip to Mars. Elite troopers are boarding the rockets as we speak, to blast off in 48 hours. While we hope that force will not be needed, we must ensure that Mars is taken back for the people of Earth.

"My thoughts go out to all those lottery winners on Mars who bravely risked their lives to create a new cradle of humanity," she continued.

"But as we seek to win the peace on Mars, we must also maintain it on Earth. We are therefore ordering a night curfew from 9pm around the planet until this period of uncertainty has passed."

***

Commander Davey waited for the Council to fall silent. The leaders of the administrative divisions stretched down the narrow table, their heads twisted attentively in her direction. She had been elected leader within weeks of arriving on the planet after promising to make Mars self-sufficient within a year.

"Following the broadcast, Earth has been in contact about the future government of our planet," she said. "They are using the threat of force to try to compel us to hand over the colony. Accepting their terms would be appeasement, and it's something we could never consider."

The councillors thumped the table spontaneously in support, and it started to resonate like a drum. After a few seconds, the commander raised her hand, and the applause slowly subsided.

"Mars must be run by Martians," she said, which led to more table thumping.

"Thank you," she said, again raising her hand. "Let us then consider the first item on the agenda – Defending Mars against Earth's Imperialists."

Jim Jameson, the green-eyed Head of Mars Defence, was first to speak. "Our assessment is they could never risk a direct attack on the dome, it's far too fragile," he said. "Even a single bullet could cause it to depressurise catastrophically. It would be suicide for the entire colony."

"That may be true, but they don't need to go that far," said the Head of Internal Security, a short, broad shouldered man with ginger hair. "They could simply block our supplies, starve us all to death."

"Don't be ridiculous - the Lots would die too, and that would be the end of the space programme," said Commander Davey. "We need to be realistic, though," she added. "It would be far better for everyone if we let them take over the colony without a fight. Then, once our new home is complete, it should be easy enough to take it back."

"And, what of the Lots?" asked Jameson.

"We need to get them on side," said the commander.

Chapter 15: New conditions

"The siren hasn't gone off," said Sally after barging into our dorm. "It should have rung out 10 minutes ago."

"And there are no guards," I said, sitting on my bed. It was eerily quiet.

We headed to the canteen at the usual time for breakfast. A few minutes later, the guards arrived wearing soft berets instead of their usual hard hats and began chatting to us like old friends.

"There's been some changes," said a lanky one, called Alex, who came to our table.

"Council has reset your working day to eight hours. There's an official notice about it," he added, handing out a fist full of leaflets:

"Following the discovery of the sinkhole, which promises new prospects for all, Mars Council has ordered a reset of working conditions. From today, your work starts at 9am and ends at 5pm. Let us rejoice at the discovery and work together to build a new home fit for the people of Mars.

"What sort of game is this?" I said to Sally.

"It's all rather predictable," she said.

"And how is that?" I asked.

"It's pressure from Earth," she said. "They are trying to appease them."

"It isn't genuine then? We could be back to working 14 hours a day just like that," I said, clicking my fingers.

"You're right," she said. "And the greatest danger will come when the new dome is complete. When the colony is self-sufficient. They won't need our cooperation after that."

"Let's strike now, then," I said. "Take destiny into our own hands. There are more than a thousand of us now, and just 500 Space Corps. These shovels are a match for any weapons they have."

I held up my spade. It was around four foot long with a sharpened edge for extra purchase on the Martian rock.

"These would be more deadly at close quarters than a bayonet," I said. "What chance would they have? A few tasers aren't going to stop five hundred Lots with pikes and shovels."

She shook her head. "We wait," she said. "They control the oxygen in all three domes. They could easily suffocate us unless we time things just right."

"And when will that be?" I asked.

"The sinkhole will have its own oxygen supply, so whoever lives there will control it," she said. "We should make our move when we're producing enough food to survive."

On Sally's recommendation, the union ordered us to cooperate in building the new dome. With the foundation posts in place, we set to work bolting together the lattice structure, which began to envelop the sinkhole like a spider's web. Once that frame was complete, we began to fix the clear panels into position. And piece by hexagonal piece, the dome started to take shape in the dusty Martian desert, like a giant Roman cathedral.

John oversaw the operation. He drove from place to place organising meetings and handing out orders. "Once you've finished your quota of work, you can take the rest of the day off," he said as the project neared completion. It made us feel human again.

With just a few pieces of the jigsaw left, the dome was shaped like half a chicken's egg pushed into the sand. The elongated design was much stronger than using a circular dome, John said. It reduced the risk of collapse.

The guards stopped patrolling, giving us new freedom to hold union meetings in the Lots' dome. And we started to enjoy life. We even invented a form of low gravity football using a super heavy ball, although heading it was outlawed because the extra momentum could knock you out. We heard nothing about negotiations with Earth. Officially there were none.

"According to my calculations, we are just four weeks from completing the dome's structure," said John at a union meeting. "Then begins the process of increasing the oxygen and nitrogen content. If all goes to plan, we'll have a breathable atmosphere in about four months' time."

"When can we plant crops?" asked Sally.

"The desalination plants are in place. So as soon as the oxygen levels are high enough, we can start operating the farm."

It was a chicken and egg situation. Mars' atmosphere provided plenty of carbon dioxide for photosynthesis, but plants need oxygen for respiration at night.

"Here's the thing," John added. "The Space Corps has set an absolute deadline of six months for the first crops. Everything possible is being done to meet that timescale."

"It sounds like they are expecting visitors," I said. "Ones that blasted off after the broadcast."

"The timescale is just about right," said Sally. "So, you could be onto something."

"Perhaps we should sabotage the dome, so we don't meet the deadline, if that's what the Space Corps wants?" I added.

"Quite the opposite," said John. "We need to hit that deadline just as much as the Space Corps."

"John is right, George," said Sally. "On this occasion our interests are aligned. We keep working flat out to meet the targets and hope that we get visitors too."

Once the last panels were assembled, six giant cryogenic pumps were rolled into position, their pipes and coils ready to freeze the Martian air into its constituents, then pump oxygen and nitrogen into the sink hole.

We watched the first machine being switched on. It groaned into life, sucking in the atmosphere and belching gases into our new home.

The pumps worked night and day for weeks, before we got word that the dome had been successfully pressurised.

The moment was marked by a visit from Commander Davey, wearing full Space Corps regalia - a white suit with gold trim on her shoulders. As we assembled inside the new dome and breathed Martian air for the first time, the Space Corps' band began to play the Mars anthem, which the commander had commissioned. None of us sang along.

"This is a giant leap for the colony," said Commander Davey, speaking with her back to the shore of the black briny lake. "It's at times like this that we need to remember how far we have come. Whatever setbacks we've had, we have made tremendous progress."

Our new home was brightly lit by the midday sun as she spoke. She adjusted her cap to keep it out of her eyes.

"The history books will record this day as a new chapter for humanity," she added. "This lake will be our life blood, and these shores will be our home.

"But while we marvel at what we have achieved, the next stage will be just as challenging. We shall prepare the ground for food production, so that soon we can fulfil our destiny of being self-sufficient."

A couple of days later, we started to move our belongings from the old dome to our new home, and pitched tents to live in.

The sinkhole was cone shaped, descending from a relatively narrow opening at the top, to a wide expanse below, with the lake situated in the middle.

"You'll have the honour of mapping the edge of the cave," said Sally as we put up a tent. "We need to know every nook and cranny in case we get in a fight. Call it an insurance card if you like."

I was thrilled to be given the chance. I gathered a small team, and we trudged clockwise along the shore. There was a cartologist to map the shoreline, a geologist and a climber.

As we set out, a brilliant shard of light lit our way. But it quickly dimmed as the sun moved across the relatively small opening of the sinkhole, and we were forced to light up our torches.

After a few hundred metres, the geologist pointed towards a pile of rocks ahead of us.

"Those rocks look like a collapsed cave," he said. We quickly clambered over them and looked inside.

"It's a lava tube," said the geologist.

We walked slowly along a tunnel, which was about eight feet high and twelve feet wide, crunching bits of Martian rock underneath our boots, until we came to a deep crevasse.

"This is far enough," I said. "We can explore more another day."

Chapter 16: Comms plan

"It's quite obvious that Mars are playing us for fools," said the Chancellor of the Exchequer for the World Government. He was a big man. So big that he could barely fit into the standard issue armchairs supplied for the meeting. "They will say whatever we want to hear, just so long as we are fool enough to send supplies," he added, shuffling uncomfortably in his seat.

The World President was taking views on the latest communications from Mars, which reported improved working conditions for Lots, and a pledge to govern the colony more fairly.

"The anarchists continue to swell in numbers despite Starforce setting sail," said the thin faced Minister for Global Security. "There are widespread calls for the space programme to be scrapped, and the funds to be used here on Earth."

"But without the programme, all hope for our species will be lost," said the Minister for Colonising Mars. "Earth would become completely ungovernable."

"Let's take a step back," said the Chancellor. "The programme looks increasingly fanciful. The sinkhole is a great discovery, but not a game changer.

"More and more supplies will need to be sent to the planet to feed the colony as it grows. It's clear that we need to consider a scaled down version. In a way that keeps faith to the colony, but allows us to divert funds to Earth where they are so badly needed."

"But all the behavioural studies show that people must believe they have a chance of getting off this planet. A scaled down version simply won't do that," said the Minister for Colonising Mars

"That's all based on pure pseudo-science," said the World President. "We've never had a situation like this, so their guess is as good as ours. How long before the troopers land?" she asked, turning to the Head of Starforce.

"Just three weeks," he said. "They are ready to take whatever action we order."

"There's only a few dozen of them," said the Minister for Global Security. "What can they possibly do against 500 Space Corps?"

"These are very tough men and women, believe me," said the Head of Starforce. "The Space Corps won't want to take them on."

"I have great faith in both the programme and the troopers," said the World President. "Once they've taken over, though, we'll need some good news from the lottery winners. Let's get a communications plan together for when they land."

Chapter 17: Star Troopers

Four spaceships carrying troopers hovered over the ground a mile to the east of the Space Corps Dome and lowered gently towards the rocky terrane. Starforce weren't taking any chances by landing too close.

"Go, go, go," yelled Corporal Torrance as the door opened and his troopers poured out of the craft, before fanning out over the dusty terrane.

Torrance was broad, blond and proud that he could strike a golf ball farther than any other man in Starforce, something he'd repeatedly reminded the crew about on the journey from Earth.

The men liked him. He could be funny, although he was prone to going over the top when larking about, which could get him into trouble with his superiors. He followed the troopers out, clambered over a pile of rocks and dropped to one knee, his low velocity rifle pointing at an imagined enemy. It had been specially designed for Mars duties, firing projectiles similar to plastic bullets used in policing on Earth. They could be deadly at short range but couldn't punch holes in the domes.

"Stay in formation," he barked, as the men snaked towards the Space Corps Dome.

As they approached it, all forty-eight troopers spread out 50 metres either side of the entrance, where they waited, ready for their orders.

The airlock of the dome swished open, and Commander Davey stepped out waving a white flag. "Good morning, gentlemen, they'll be no need for guns," she said. "Welcome to Mars, we have refreshments waiting for you."

"Where's Hodges?" said Captain Rossiter, stepping out from behind one of the troopers, his handlebar moustache twisted upwards into points, clearly visible through his visor. "We need to speak to him asap."

***

He interviewed me in the officers' mess. Coming from the dank, dusky sinkhole, I was struck by its splendour. Paintings of famous spaceships adorned the walls, with signed portraits of their illustrious captains underneath. A sumptuous, chequered carpet lined the floor, and two fake crystal chandeliers hung from a decorated plasterboard ceiling.

"Sit here, please," said Captain Rossiter, as we got to one of the many tables that filled the long room. "You made quite an impression on Earth with your broadcast," he added.

"We did wonder if it got through," I said. "The Space Corps said they were able to edit it before it was broadcast."

"They were lying," he said. "We were sent to sort things out because of it."

I pulled out a chair from under the table and sat down.

"So why do you want to speak to me?" I asked.

"Because I think we can trust you to tell us what's been happening," he said. "We're in control now, so you don't have to worry about what you say."

"Don't trust them," I told him. "No matter what they do, don't trust them an inch. That's what I've learned about them."

"Well, at least they had the good sense to submit to my troopers," he said. "It's the most sensible thing they've done in months. Though it's an act of supreme self-preservation, of course."

I briefed him on how conditions had worsened since I'd arrived at the red planet, then improved in the months after the transmission. That Commander Davey was their leader and Sally was ours.

"We'll need to fix you up with a connection to Earth, so you can start your reports again," he said.

I relished the prospect of writing regular news bulletins once more but had lost faith with Martin.

"I'll put the media distribution list together, if you don't mind," I said.

"Go for it," he said. "Just copy me into the articles, so I can see what you've been saying. I'll need to speak to Sally next. But it's getting late, and I must speak to my troopers. Let's meet here at sparrows' farts tomorrow."

Our convoy left for the sinkhole at first light. Corporal Torrance slammed his foot on the accelerator, and the transporter jumped into action, bouncing up and down on the well-worn track to our new home. He slammed the brakes at the entrance, and we came to an abrupt halt, the other vehicles lining up quietly next to us.

"Wow, that's an impressive building," said Captain Rossiter as we got out. "There's something about the curves that remind me of Sydney Opera House," he grinned. "It's going to be a postcard one day, for sure. What's it like here at night?"

"Phobos will blow your mind as it traces across the sky," I said. "But you're going to miss seeing Earth's Moon in the sky. The Milky Way is extra bright here on Mars, though, so it's never truly dark."

Unlike the rest of us, the troopers had a return ticket to Earth. Their spaceships were busily converting water and carbon dioxide into oxygen and methane needed for the journey, using a complex series of chemical reactions. It would take a few months, but their tanks would eventually have enough fuel to make the journey home.

At the entrance, I tapped in a code and the airlock clunked open. I unlatched the escalator doors and slid them apart. They folded like a concertina and four of us stepped inside. An electric motor whirled into action, and we descended smoothly to the shore, before stopping with a bump.

"You can take your helmets off now," I said, as we stepped out into the sinkhole.

Captain Rossiter unbuckled his helmet and tucked it under his arm.

"Sweet as," he said, sucking in the air.

Teams of Lots were busily assembling buildings in the village and hauling equipment to the farm.

"It's quite incredible," the captain said. "The Public Relations team on Earth will die for pictures of this. But all in good time."

He made a beeline for the lake. When we got there, he crouched down at the edge and dipped his hand in the water.

"What's in it?" he asked, as the water dripped from his fingers.

"Very high levels of minerals," I said. "It would be very risky to drink it. In fact, we're telling people to steer clear of the lake for now, until we've done some more tests. It's at least 50 metres deep though."

"And what's the oxygen level in the air down here?" he asked, standing up again.

"Twenty-one percent, the same as Earth," I said. "Cryogenic machines automatically fine-tune the air twenty-four hours a day. As long as they keep working, it will be perfect."

"They are nuclear powered, aren't they," he said. "That means they will need to be replaced one day."

"They'll have enough power for hundreds of years, if not thousands," I said. "And hopefully we'll have terraformed the planet or found another power source by then."

We walked along the water's edge to the farm, where a team of Lots were tending to some hydroponic trays, which were stacked in rows ten feet high. "Amazing. What are you growing?" he asked, casting an eye down the long stretch of shore where the farm was being assembled.

"Rice, beans and beets are the main crops," I said. "Yields have improved since we introduced dwarf varieties. Given the size of the farm, we should have enough food to feed the entire colony, with room to produce much more, if need be."

"Are there any more sinkholes?" he asked. "This one will be full in a few years."

"None have been found. But it seems unlikely that it's the only one," I said. "We're not thinking too far ahead."

We walked past a line of green tents towards a dozen half-built bungalows.

"What are you making these bricks from?" he asked.

"It turns out that Martian dust makes pretty good ones," I said, tapping a wall with my boot. "The first of these permanent houses will be ready in a few weeks' time."

The village had been mapped out with flag poles showing where hundreds of new dwellings would be built. It was going to be a kilometre long and half a kilometre wide. A road would run through the centre, with more streets leading like spokes to houses.

"Are any of the Space Corps living with you down here?" he asked.

"No, it's just us Lots," I said. "It's very much 'them and us' and it seems they prefer their living quarters."

We reached a large round house being built at the centre of the village. "This will be the communal building," I said. "Somewhere we can meet and socialise."

"Do you have a long-term plan for the village," he asked. "A strategic plan?"

"We haven't got anything like that, we just get things signed off by the union and Mars Council on a day-to-day basis," I said.

The captain frowned. "You'll need a long-term plan, or something will come and bite you on the arse."

"I really don't think it's necessary," I said, slapping him on the back as we walked to join the others. "After all, what could be harder than dealing with the Space Corps?"

Chapter 18: New beginnings

"Congratulations, Sandy, you're pregnant," said Joe, the blond-haired medic.

Sandy looked at the faint blue lines on the test kit, which confirmed she was having a baby, and passed it to her partner, Tony. His face beamed. Mars' first baby was on its way.

"I'd say you are about three months' pregnant," Joe added.

"How big is it?" asked Tony.

"It's about the size of a broad bean," said Joe.

When Sandy told me the news, I was delighted. But in less than a fortnight, three more couples had positive tests.

"We could have dozens of children in the camp by this time next year at this rate," I told Sally.

"It's because of our new home," she said. "People can envisage raising children here. The whole colony is young, and without any children. It's bound to happen."

"We'll need to build a maternity unit, and a school," I said. "I don't even know if we've got a midwife."

"Don't worry," she said. "We have several doctors, and midwifery is part of their training. I'll let them know what's happening."

Chapter 19: Message from Mars

My hands trembled as I leafed through the script. Parts of it felt rather glib, but Captain Rossiter was determined to have a good news story, and who was I to disagree? After all, he'd saved the colony.

"Counting down, 5,4,3,2,1 rolling," said the camera operator.

"Good day to the people of Earth from the people of Mars, as we greet you from the shores of the Badwater Lake," I said, pointing a hand in the direction of the glistening black water beside me. Captain Rossiter and I were sitting on chairs with a coffee table at our feet, in an attempt to look like breakfast television on Earth.

"I am delighted to be joined by Captain Rossiter who touched down with the rest of Starforce yesterday. Captain, please tell us about what happened after you landed," I said, turning to him.

"Thank you, George," he said. "Everything went to plan. The troopers touched down at exactly 9am. We were given a friendly welcome by the Space Corps, and they handed over the administration of the colony under emergency powers set out on Earth."

A crowd of Lots had gathered behind the camera operator to watch the broadcast. I could hear them chatting as the captain spoke.

"It's been great to meet you and so many of the lottery winners since we arrived," he continued. "Perhaps you could tell people on Earth how your life has changed since your last broadcast?"

"Well, we saw some quite dramatic changes within a few weeks," I said. "Our working conditions were reset to eight hours a day with weekends restored. Rations were increased, and the guards were gradually withdrawn from around us."

"So, how would you describe morale among the Lots now?" he asked.

"Morale is quite good," I said. "We are being treated well."

"And tell us a little bit more about your work on the sinkhole?" he asked.

"We are building a village by the shore," I said. "It's a spectacular achievement. The sinkhole has a breathable atmosphere – something we thought impossible on the Mars' surface.

"We have machines that suck in the oxygen and nitrogen from Mars' atmosphere and pump it into the sinkhole 24 hours a day. And the farm is producing enough staple foods to feed us…"

Chapter 20: New charter

"Come to my tent to discuss our approach to tomorrow's ceremony," read Sally's email. She was referring to the signing of a 'Bill of Rights for the People of Mars,' being organised by Captain Rossiter. Emanating from Earth, the bill had been circulated to everyone on Mars earlier that morning. It was to be signed the very next day by Mars Council and the Lots' union.

I rushed to Sally's tent. John was already there, reading the manuscript at rapid speed. He had the unnerving ability to scan documents twice as fast as everyone else, which always put him one step ahead.

"It's a fait accompli," said Sally, offering me a seat next to her. "But it looks good for us; it has everything we could want," she added.

"Such as?" I asked.

"For starters, there's a right to a trial by a jury of your peers, and the right to vote in free and fair elections every year. There's also the right to freedom of speech, and a system of proportional representation for the Mars Council."

"The Space Corps will hate that," I said. "They'll be voted out of power at the very first election."

"No one was consulted, least of all the Space Corps," said John, looking up from the thirty-page manuscript. "I'm not sure how they will react? I can't see any mention of power sharing."

"This isn't South Africa," I said. "They won't get reserved ministries just because they are the Space Corps."

"They will have to sign," added Sally. "They are over a barrel. If the commander doesn't agree, the bill will be guillotined into law by Earth anyway. John, tell the others that we are backing the new constitution."

He left, leaving Sally and me to celebrate.

She opened a bottle of bootleg rice wine and showed me around her bungalow. It was decorated like a Parisienne dream house, with Mars standard issue curtains creatively fashioned into drapes, and the plastic flooring painted to look like white boarding. Her hall was dusky pink, with a spare bedroom turned into a luxurious dressing room.

"Welcome to my sanctuary," she said, as we toured the rooms. "I can't tell you how happy it makes me to have a space of my own after all this time in dorms."

"You've got a flair for design," I said. Our eyes met momentarily in the dimmed light. "I must do something more with mine."

"I can help you do that," she said as we sat down on the sofa. "I'm not sure this ceremony is going to be as straight forward as the troopers think," she added.

"Nothing on this planet is straight forward, but I'm happier now than at any time since I arrived," I said.

"Me too, George," she said.

***

Hundreds of Lots were milling around in the community hall as we arrived for the signing ceremony the next morning. The building was freshly plastered and the roof was on, but electric wires poked out of walls and some floorboards still needed nailing down. A pile of them lay in one corner.

Corporal Torrance spotted Sally and me from across the room and ushered us to the main table. It was set on a stage overlooking the audience. "Please take your seats," he said, sitting us down quickly. Opposite, looking pensive, was Commander Davey. Gone was the gold regalia, replaced with a standard issue Lot boiler suit.

"Good morning, Commander," I said, trying not to look too smug. "It's a huge day for the colony."

"Time to put the past behind us," she said.

There were two dozen of us at the table. At the centre was Corporal Torrance and Captain Rossiter who were flanked by armed troopers. I could see a handful more troopers milling about the room, watching the proceedings carefully.

"Ladies and gentlemen of Mars," said Captain Rossiter finally. "My troopers and I have been working closely with leaders from right across the colony to prepare for a new phase in Mars' history. One which gives equal rights to all, whether you are a lottery winner or a space corps officer.

"I am delighted, then, to gather here with you today to sign the new charter, which will enshrine those rights in law."

"Hear, hear," said Sally, as applause rang out around the hall.

"But let's consider the charter for a moment," he added. "It sets out the legal framework for how the colony will be governed from this day forward.

"Earth will continue to hold some executive functions, but a new system of democracy will allow the colony to evolve according to its own needs, and at its own pace."

Applause rang out again. I glanced at the commander who remained poker faced.

"Time for talking is over, let us sign the new charter into law," said Captain Rossiter, handing it to Commander Davey. She signed her name quickly and passed it to Sally, who added hers. The document was passed from person to person until everyone around the table had signed. I was rather exuberant, my scribble taking up the whole of one corner.

"Congratulations, ladies and gentlemen," said Captain Rossiter. "I welcome you to the new Mars."

Chapter 21: Trap

"Strangled," gasped John after barging into Sally's bungalow. "They've strangled the troopers as they slept in their beds."

I was standing in the kitchen with her, wearing just my pyjamas. He was taken aback for a moment at seeing us together, but quickly recovered his composure.

"How many?" asked Sally, sitting down slowly at the breakfast table.

"All the troopers in the Space Corps dome," he said, glancing at me. "Forty must be dead."

"What about the others?" I asked.

"They were bunking in one of the spaceships," he said. "They're fighting a pitched battle with the Space Corps as we speak. But they're heavily outnumbered – at least ten to one, and the Space Corps has guns now."

"We must do something to help," I said. "If they go down, so does the colony."

"They will try to head this way," said Sally. "It's their only chance."

"The Space Corps is blocking them," said John.

I couldn't bear the thought of leaving the remaining troopers to their fate. "Let's round up a hundred volunteers and attack the Corps from the rear," I said. "We can take them out in a pincer movement."

"We'd be mown down in seconds," said John. "And we don't have time. The fight will be over by the time we get there."

"Let's set up our defences here then," said Sally, before heading to her room to get changed.

"I'll set up a greeting party," I said, doing the same. Fearing the worst, I dictated a report on voicemail and sent it to my distribution list on Earth without a thought:

Title: Troopers strangled in their sleep

Strapline: Battle rages after Space Corps attacks troopers

Main body: Troopers are battling the Space Corps after dozens were strangled to death as they slept in their beds, according to witnesses.

Lots are setting up defences at the sinkhole as the remaining troopers battle with the Space Corps in the Mars desert...

I rushed out of Sally's cottage and ran about camp calling for volunteers. When I had a dozen, we suited up as quickly as we could, grabbed some pikes and scrambled to the lifts. Outside, we stacked sandbags into a barricade and crouched down with our weapons ready.

Chapter 22: Battle stations

"Mayday, Mayday, Mayday," blasted over the two-way radio.

Captain Rossiter jumped out of his bed like a scalded cat.

"What's happening, trooper? Over," said the captain, his hands clutching at the transmitter.

"We were attacked as we slept, most of the troopers dead – strangled. Over," crackled the voice through the transmitter.

"What's your situation now, trooper? Over," said Captain Rossiter, as he paced around the spacecraft.

"Hopeless. Just three of us left. We're making a last stand in the Space Corps mess. Running low on ammunition."

He let out a blood curdling scream and the radio fell silent.

"Are you there, trooper? Over," barked the captain, but there was just a crackle.

A massive blast knocked him off his feet.

"Abandon ship," he ordered, suiting up as quickly as he could. He pulled the emergency exit lever, and shoots unfurled to the ground below.

"Rendezvous at the transporters," he ordered, pushing out a trooper, who slid down the chute and crashed onto the surface below.

When there was no one left inside, the captain grabbed a gun and jumped for it, landing on top of one of the men.

"Get up trooper," he shouted, pulling him to his feet. An explosion blew out the feet of the rocket, and it started to wobble.

"Get clear of the ship," yelled the captain, as it came crashing down like a dynamited Victorian tower. The troopers were up and running now, their guns firing at a squad of Space Corps officers facing them. The Space Corps formed into a defensive line. They were using hexagonal dome panels as shields. The captain fired a bullet. It bounced off harmlessly.

"Fix bayonets," he ordered, then "charge," and all eight troopers rushed forward.

The Space Corps hurled a volley of pikes as they approached. One struck a trooper, ripping his space suit open.

He writhed around on the ground in agony as air gushed out. Moments later, the troopers clattered into the Space Corps, their bayonets ripping through suits and bodies. It did the trick, they scattered.

"Rendezvous at the sinkhole," ordered Captain Rossiter, as he desperately tried to patch up the injured trooper's space suit with some tape. It worked, and they lugged him onto a transporter.

"Let's go," said Captain Rossiter, and they sped off at full speed, leaving the Space Corps in their dust.

As they approached the sinkhole, the captain could see us manning the barricades. "Thank god," he said. "Let's get the injured trooper inside."

Chapter 23: Riots

"A dramatic development at the Mars colony," said Sandra, sitting on the couch at breakfast television. "Dozens of troopers were strangled last night as they slept in their beds, according to a message from Mars.

"The voicemail, which was sent an hour ago by Mars journalist George Hodges, says a pitched battle between the remaining troopers and the Space Corps was taking place on the surface of Mars.

"We have reached out to the World Government for comment but have not yet received a response."

"And now for a message," she added as the channel went to adverts.

Tom stared at the screen in disbelief.

"It's crazy - people are starving in the streets while they spend trillions building houses on a planet run by homicidal maniacs," he said. "We've got to stop it."

"It's up to us to do something, man," said one of his friends from the radical Action Today Party. Half a dozen of them were sitting in a dingy flat, smoking a badly packed spliff.

"We need to force their hand," said Tom. "This is our moment."

"People are gathering at spaceports," said the long-haired friend, taking a deep puff before passing the spliff to an outstretched hand. "We should go there and help," he spluttered, trying not to breathe out too quickly.

Tom got to his feet. "I'm going, is anyone with me?" he said. But his friends just groaned. "Yeah, man, maybe after we've finished this spliff," said one of them lying motionless on a couch.

Tom jumped to his feet and rushed down a flight of steps to his car. He drove at top speed to the Cornish Space Port, excited at the prospect of joining the action. He weaved his way through burning cars and looted shops, until he was stopped by gridlocked traffic, five miles from the port. Abandoning his car, he began to walk the rest of the journey, then broke into a jog as he dodged through the crowds to get to the launch site.

"Fascists out! Fascists out!" rang out around him. He saw a woman scream "Fascist pig!" at a policeman, her face centimetres from the officer's. The policeman remained composed, looking her cooly in the eyes, as she pushed her red face closer and closer towards his.

Along with thousands of others intent on venting their fury, Tom surged through the perimeter of the space port.

The mob were vandalising everything in their path, ripping up signs, trampling over car bonnets. Finally, he was at the front, where the mob were baying at the thin blue line facing them. The police were bashing their battens rhythmically against their shields. In response, the protesters hurled cans and rocks across an eight-foot fence that separated the two tribes. The mob surged forward, grabbing the fence's mesh wire and started to yank it. Tom started to pull and push with the others, and it began to sway violently back and forth on its fixings, swinging ever more wildly. Back and forth it went for several minutes until the concrete posts snapped and the protestors surged over.

"Aim, fire!" screeched the commanding officer, and a volley of rubber bullets took out a dozen protesters. A woman next to Tom took one to the head. She fell to the floor and was trampled by the throng of protestors pouring forward.

"Fire!" came another command, and a second row of protestors went down. Bodies piled up as people clambered over the injured to get to the police.

"Fire at will!" came the command, and dozens more rubber bullets smashed into the crowd.

A water cannon opened-up, forcing the protestors back momentarily. Then another two cannons let rip, causing more people to topple over.

But there were too many of them. Tom grappled a police officer and was battered backwards by a truncheon. His arm smashed in the fight.

He watched in horror as a protestor pulled out a knife and stabbed a policeman in the shoulder. Two more officers battered the knifeman to the floor.

The police began to retreat, firing volley after volley of rubber bullets as they did so.

"Live fire," rang out. Then. "Fire at will."

But it was too late. The mob overran the line, and the police ran for it. Some of the rioters gave chase, others ransacked the spaceport, setting fire to the control centre and lighting great pyres under the spaceships being readied for flight.

It was two hours before the crowd began to melt away. Tom was one of the last to go. "The spaceport is destroyed," he shouted to anyone listening. "Victory."
***

The World President watched in horror as attacks spread across the globe.

"Eight hundred police officers killed and 20,000 protestors dead or injured, are the latest figures," said the Minister for Global Security. "Sixty percent of world spaceports destroyed or damaged," he added.

"Where's the army?" demanded the World President.

"They haven't deployed in the numbers we'd hoped for, Ms President," said the Minister.

"It's over," she said, cradling her head in her hands. "We're going to have to cancel the programme."
***

"We just wanted to say how much we admire you, Tom," came a sultry voice down the prison telephone. Ruth, the Members' Secretary of the Action Today Party, was speaking to him from her Kensington home.

"Thanks, it's just nice to hear a friendly voice," said Tom. "How on earth did you get past the screws?"

"I just told him it was my job to try to speak to you, and that I'd keep trying until he told me in no uncertain terms to 'bugger off.' I came straight through to you after that."

"I'm impressed, that was Mallard you spoke to - he's the toughest screw in the prison."

"Not so tough really, I think," said Ruth. "How are things going?"

"Not great. They've put me in isolation for six weeks, until I get transferred to a lower category prison. I've got a price on my head because the bosses said I grassed them up. Everyone knows it's a lie but that makes no odds in prison."

"That's terrible," said Ruth.

There was an awkward pause while she tried to think of something to say.

"None of us could believe the sentence, Tom. Ten years for a protest, it's so unfair," she said finally.

"They're making an example of us protesters. The main thing is we won," he said.

"Did you hear about the money from the Space Corps programme?" she asked nervously, wondering whether he'd heard the news.

"No," he said. "What's happened?"

"They've diverted it to defence and security because of the riots."

Tom's heart sank.

"But you can be assured that we are doing everything we can to get it spent on the starving," she added. "We've got a sponsored cycle ride this weekend to raise funds for a campaign."

"What a disaster," said Tom, holding his head in his hands.

Chapter 24: Legion

After taking his injured man to the medical bay, Captain Rossiter's first step was to take an inventory of arms.

"Eight guns, 200 pikes, 200 shields and 200 spades," I said, after compiling a list of the equipment he'd asked for.

"Not as much as I'd hoped," said Rossiter, inspecting the weapons, which I'd neatly stored next to the escalator as requested.

"We have almost 2,100 Lots against just 500 Space Corps," said John. "I'd say that gives us the advantage."

"Poor analysis," said the captain. "How many weapons do they have?"

"About the same as us, I'd estimate," said John.

"On the battlefield then, the numbers will be even," said Captain Rossiter. "But we do have one advantage."

"What's that?" asked Sally. "You, I suppose?"

She seemed less impressed by the captain's manly bravado than the rest of us.

"You guessed it," he smiled. "Me and the other troopers. The Space Corps don't have anyone with military training."

"We're not fighting with tanks and machine guns now, captain," she said.

"The military tactics remain the same," he said. "But this battle will be fought like Romans against the barbarians. And I have until dawn to turn you rabble into centurions."

One of his troopers approached with news of our defences above. "The Space Corps have pulled back to their dome," he said.

"Congratulations, George," said Captain Rossiter slapping my shoulder. "Your defences held. The Space Corps were easily frightened, but it won't be long before they summon the courage to come back. And in greater numbers no doubt."

"You'd better get a move on training us then," said Sally.

"The first step will be to assemble the Lots by the lake," he said. "In the next half hour would be good."

We strode about camp, calling for everyone to make their way to an assembly point on the far side of the lake, where the shore was at its widest. Nearly the whole camp was waiting when the captain arrived.

"Some time in the next hours or days, the Space Corps will come to fight us for this sinkhole," he said, trying to stir them. "And to win the battle, we will need to fight like Romans."

The Lots looked at each other, slightly bemused.

He held out an eight-foot pike. "The Roman soldier was armed with just a javelin, short sword and a shield," he said. "But he conquered most of the known world. We have shields, pikes and spades. How can we win? With iron discipline and smart military tactics. I need a legion of two hundred soldiers to face them, who's with me?"

A huge roar resonated around the sinkhole.

"I need only the strongest and bravest of you," he continued, throwing me a pike. I picked it up and held it by my side.

"If you can throw that pike over those rocks, you're in," he said, pointing to an outcrop by the lake about 100 yards away.

With a brisk run up, I launched it with all my might. It sailed high over the rocks and thudded into the side of the sinkhole.

"You're in," said the captain.

The Lots lined up to take turns. Some threw much farther than me, others fell short. Those selected waited next to the lake, while the others made their way back to camp.

When the captain had two hundred volunteers, he called an end to it. "Enough," he said. "Now gather round and I'll teach you how to fight."

He handed me an hexagonal shield. I grabbed its handles, which had been screwed into place, and positioned it just below eye level.

"Now pick up a shovel," said the captain.

I held it in my right hand, with the handle running along my forearm like a trident.

"Hold it close to your side and try to stab with it," he said.

When I was set, he rushed towards me, clattering me off balance with his shield.

"You strike here, or here, for a kill," he said, jabbing towards my neck and solar plexus.

"If you strike here, or here, you'll inflict a mortal wound," he added, pointing towards my stomach and crutch. "And a blow to the lower legs or feet will immobilise your opponent," he said, scything his shovel across my ancles. "But here's the most important thing you will hear me say today. You must stand shoulder to shoulder with your comrades, or we will lose the tactical advantage. It will protect you against attack from the flanks."

We were split into five cohorts of 40 fighters and sent away to practice. I led the gold cohort, John green, Sally red. The captain briefed us on battle tactics as the soldiers trained with shields and spades.

"We will use the slope outside the sinkhole to our advantage, so we can fight the enemy from higher ground," he said. "Three cohorts will engage them front on, with two more behind acting as reinforcements, to plug any gaps during the fight. My troopers will use the transporters like cavalry, to protect the wings."

He showed the legion how to position their shields to protect against a volley of pikes thrown like javelins. Soldiers at the front held their shields vertically, while those behind raised theirs above their heads.

"Just before we engage, launch your pikes and then crash into the enemy lines with your shields," he told them. "Then stab with your spades. I know you can do it."

I gulped at the thought of going into battle. Keeping to formation was asking a lot.

"Our scouts will give warning if they attack tonight," he added. "But, for now, get some sleep."

Chapter 25: Slime

The sun rose the next day, casting a bright crescent across the top of the sinkhole, bringing an eerie light to the colony below. A few minutes later, an array of lights flickered on around the camp, signalling the start of the day.

There was a loud knock at my door - it was Sally. My heart raced.

"There's been a major discovery in the lava tube," she said. "It looks like some form of life."

I should have been more amazed, but I just felt flat.

"What on earth is it?" I asked.

"Don't get too excited, it's just a red goo. Come and take a look."

A metal door had been installed at the cave's entrance. Sally tapped in a code, and it clunked open. "It's the first five prime numbers," she said.

A lot had happened since we had discovered the lava tube. It was a hub of activity, with dozens of Lots walking in and out of the chamber. There were crates of medical provisions and boxes of canned food stacked next to the walls of the tunnel.

"You have been busy," I said. "What are all these people doing?"

"We've started mapping the lava tubes," she said. "They fan out in all directions. The temperature increases the further you go in. We've got a team of scientist researching the slime."

We walked across a bridge spanning the chasm we'd stopped at weeks earlier, and into a small cave on one side.

"It's really disgusting," said Sally, pointing a torch at the slime, which quivered under the light. An odour of rotten eggs filled the space. "Our best guess is it's some kind of bacteria."

"Can we eat it?" I asked.

"That's the question," she said. "John is analysing a sample, so we should know more in a few days."

I cut a bit off with my knife and took a closer look. It looked solid, but was liquid around the edges where the knife had cut through. I ran my knife along the wall.

"It's bleeding," I said, watching liquid ooze out.

We took a step back to get away from the pong. "It doesn't smell very appetising," I said.

"It's probably poisonous," she said. "But perhaps we could process it into something edible."

"That would be the answer to our prayers," I said. "But how are you going to test it?"

"We'll do it the way our ancestors did when they found something new to eat. They'd try a tiny piece first and then wait to see if there was a reaction. Then, they'd gradually build up the portions, until they knew it was safe."

We headed back to the entrance discussing the discovery. We were confident it would help us in some way, even if we didn't know what that was yet.

"Why the airtight door?" I asked when we got to the exit.

"This is our bunker if things get tough," she said. "I'll be running some drills to get people used to assembling here."

Despite everything that had happened, I still had an audience on the home planet, and this was a huge story, so I sent a report to Earth:

A new lifeform may have been discovered on Mars

A slime found on the red planet could be a new type of bacteria, according to experts on the red planet.

The red goo was found in a cave inside the sinkhole.

Tests are being carried out to confirm whether it is a new life form.

The Lots hope it could be used to help the colony...

Chapter 26: Space Corps

"A handful of troopers slipped through our fingers," said the platoon captain, a scientist who'd had the misfortune of leading the Space Corps attack on the rocket. "They made it to the sinkhole."

Commander Davey had called him to her quarters for an update on the mission.

"What?" said the commander. "You didn't finish them off as you were ordered?"

"They are trained soldiers, Mamm," protested the captain. "They are the best of the best, while we are just scientists and engineers."

"Nonsense," said the commander. "You had many times their numbers. You have failed in your mission – there will be no second chances."

She gave a signal, and two guards grabbed him by the shoulders and dragged him away. The room watched in silence as his protests faded into the distance.

"How much food do we have?" the commander asked, finally.

"As long as the rockets keep coming, we have enough to survive," said Jameson.

"That gives us eight months to take the sinkhole," said the commander. "Earth is in flames; the space programme is over."

"We still have the farm," said the head of agriculture.

"Without the Lots? I think you overestimate your ability to grow a decent crop," said the commander.

"If we blow a hole in the sinkhole, it would be the end of the Lots," said Jameson. "We could rebuild and move in."

"An interesting proposition," said Commander Davey. "But very high-risk. It would take months to repressurise. And they might retaliate in kind."

"There is another way, that keeps the sinkhole intact," said Jameson. "A way of drawing them outside."

The commander smiled. "I can see you have a germ of an idea. Get a plan together by the end of the day."

Chapter 27: Battle of the Sinkhole

"This chow better not have any slime in it," I said to Sally the next morning, as we ate breakfast in her bungalow. I was in a surprisingly good mood considering what was about to happen.

"You'd be the ideal person to test it," she said. "The way you put your food away, your stomach would be a perfect laboratory."

Before I had a chance to reply, the battle stations siren began to bellow up and down, like a second world war air raid signal. Sally and I looked at each other for a second, then rushed outside.

We made our way to a spot near the foot of the escalator, where our space suits had been neatly laid out. Two hundred of them ready to grab, along with pikes, shields and spades. We suited up and walked to a meeting point a few metres away, where the other cohort leaders had gathered, along with Captain Rossiter and his men.

"At least two hundred enemy were spotted heading towards us a few minutes ago," he said. "We need to get out asap and assemble on the high ground. Cram your soldiers into the escalators."

The captain turned to the men and women amassing behind us. "If we can defend our home today, then we will write the history of this planet," he said. "But if we lose this battle, then a new dark chapter will follow, written by the Space Corps."

The Lots raised their pikes in the air and let out a roar. "They're ready," said Captain Rossiter.

I burst out of the escalator with a dozen soldiers from my cohort. More and more amassed outside, until all my troops were at the surface. We formed five rows of eight soldiers, facing the Space Corps. I could see clouds of dust in the distance as they slowly closed in. We marched, shoulder to shoulder, to the high ground with the captain and corporal riding either side of us in transporters.

Sally's cohort of troops assembled to our left. Then John's positioned itself on our right. The sun glinted off our shields, as we waited for the order to attack. The Space Corps formed a long line on the horizon, perhaps half a dozen soldiers thick, holding pikes and shields.

Our reserves finally got into position when the Space Corps were just 100 metres away.

Then all hell broke loose. Two Space Corps transporters rushed our lines, tyres spinning as they accelerated to ramming speed.

Captain Rossiter drove full pelt towards one, colliding with it headfirst, causing it to somersault. It landed helplessly on its back, wheels still spinning, the driver desperately trying to open its crumpled doors. The captain's vehicle was immobilised, venting steam. He got out and rushed to join us.

Corporal Torrance raced out to block the second. It swerved to miss him and fled over a hill with the corporal in pursuit.

The Space Corps started to wave their pikes in the air, like a prelude to a medieval attack. They fired their guns, reigning plastic bullets on our lines. We crouched behind our shields, and they ricocheted off. A thick fog of Martian dust started to form as hundreds of boots kicked into the soil. I gave the order to hurl our pikes, which plunged into their ranks. A few of them went down, but the main effect was to cause panic, and their lines started to separate. We charged forward and clattered into them, sending the front row flying. Then we began to systematically cut through by stabbing at the gaps between their shields.

One of them came in front of me with a pike. I aimed a blow at his chest, which slashed through his spacesuit. Then another attacked from my side, but the soldier on my right dispatched him before he could land a blow.

A pile of dead and wounded built up as the battle turned into a rout. We lost formation as we clambered over their bodies. But it didn't matter. With their backs to us, we mowed them down at will. In less than an hour, it was over. Jameson rushed back to the dome with a few of us chasing. I counted the casualties: 50 space corps dead along with six Lots.

Chapter 28: A way forward

"If this were a game of chess, I would call it stalemate," said Captain Rossiter at the debrief the next day with Sally, John and me. We were talking in the trooper's mess, a large bungalow the captain had commissioned for his men. "We won the battle, but not the war," he added.

"But surely the day is ours?" I said indignantly. "We've got the better army - we could just walk over there and take over their dome once and for all."

"It wouldn't be that easy," said the captain. "It's much harder to take a defensive position than beat an army on open terrain. And they could blow up the sinkhole in retaliation, leaving us for dead."

"And we could do the same to them," said Sally.

"Exactly. It's like a nuclear deterrent for both sides," said the captain. "A weapon of last resort, that no one wants to use."

"Then what do you suggest we do?" asked Sally.

"We're not going to negotiate."

"I'm afraid it's the only logical way forward," said John apologetically. "We must reach an agreement that accommodates everyone. They'll just get desperate if we don't, and who knows what they'll do then."

"That's out of the question," I said. "They're sure to double cross us again."

"Maybe so, but we have little choice," said the captain. "And if we get the negotiations right, we can secure our future. We can bind them into an agreement. We could get them to agree to being part of a minority Government, with us in charge. Part of the deal is they dis-arm and we run the security force. They'd be fools not to accept. As distasteful as it is, negotiations like this have happened throughout history."

***

"You got us into this mess, Jameson," said Commander Davey. "How do you propose we get out of it?"

"I'm afraid we underestimated them, commander. But there is a silver lining," he said.

"Go on, I can't wait to hear it," said the commander.

"The losses, while unfortunate, do mean that our provisions will last longer."

"You are clutching at straws," said the commander, turning away from him in disgust. "And it only prolongs the agony."

"There is one way forward," said Jameson.

"I'm listening," said the commander. "But you better get it right this time."

Chapter 29: Talks

When the offer came into our inboxes, it looked exactly like what we wanted. But there was a sting in the tail.

Offer of talks

The Space Corps is today reaching out to the Lots of Mars to offer a negotiated peace.

With supplies from Earth coming to an end, we must work together to create a sustainable future.

Rather than continue a conflict which risks all parties, we propose we agree terms favourable to all. A conference should be held to discuss the future structure of Mars' government. We propose that the Lots and Space Corps have an equal say in the future direction of the planet.

As a show of good faith, the Space Corps will free all three troopers it has held as prisoners once a settlement is agreed in principle.

"It's an olive branch," said Sally, after reading it out to the Lots' union and Captain Rossiter in the community hall.

"My men will be overjoyed about the troopers," said the captain. "But they will want them freed as soon as possible. Our motto is 'we never leave one behind,' after all."

"I'm sure everyone is delighted about the troopers," said Sally. "But we cannot let that cloud our judgement on what to do next. We can't agree to the Space Corps having an equal say. It must be one person, one vote."

One by one the union leaders gave their support to talks. The only red line was that the colony must be run as a democracy.

***

Sally organised a teleconference to discuss terms the next day. We set up a table on the stage above the main hall. Hundreds of Lots sat in chairs watching the event on a big screen. We logged into the meeting five minutes early and waited patiently for the Space Corps to appear online.

One by one, the faces of Commander Davey, John Jameson and several other Space Corps officers popped up on screen.

"Good morning, commander," said Sally. "We are pleased to accept your request to discuss terms. Let's go straight to the first point on the agenda: 'Pre-requisites for negotiations for a peaceful resolution of the conflict.'

"Point 1: Laying down of arms: the Lots require that the Space Corps hand over all their weapons as a sign of good faith."

"Chair, before we begin, I would like to comment on the agenda," said Commander Davey.

"Go ahead," said Sally.

"We have reached out to the Lots in good faith," said the commander. "But equality between the two parties must be the overriding principal in the negotiations. So, both sides of this conflict will need to show the same flexibility on arms. You can't expect just one side to hand over all their weapons, while the other does nothing."

"You did reach out to us, commander. But that was because you were routed in battle," said Sally.

I looked at the ten point agenda. It seemed hopelessly ambitious.

"May I be so bold as to offer a way forward," said Jameson.

"Go on," said Sally.

"We need to build trust, that much is clear," he said. "As a first step, we would like to invite you to send a senior delegation to the Space Corps dome, so you can see the work we are doing to increase agricultural production. There have been some major improvements, which could ultimately lead to us becoming self-sustainable."

"That's preposterous," I said. "It's a trap. We don't have to listen to this."

"We don't need to set a trap – we could just blow up your precious sinkhole if we wanted to," said Jameson.

"And we could blast your dome sky high," I said.

Sally shook her head. "I suggest we arrange another meeting when temperatures have cooled, and expectations have become a bit more realistic."

Chapter 30: Raiders

Corporal Torrance was a keen caver in his youth, and he felt the excitement of those days return as he reviewed the map of the lava tubes. They fanned out around the sinkhole like a spider's web.

"We got lucky," he told the assembled team of men. "There's a tunnel that runs directly under the Space Corps' dome. We should be able to pop our heads up in the prison cell, snatch our troopers, dynamite the tunnel and be back for breakfast."

The six troopers nodded approvingly.

The squad set off, clambering along the tunnel, with the corporal using his orienteering skills to point the way. To help retrace their steps, they laid a thin line of steel.

The tunnel forked left, then right, then opened into a chamber. Stalactites hung from the ceiling like spears in a gothic dungeon.

Corporal Torrance glanced at his temperature gage, "Thirty-five centigrade," he said. "Keep it slow and steady, lads – I don't want anyone passing out."

They crept along the tunnel for half an hour before reaching the destination.

"We are directly below the prison cell, according to the maps," said the corporal. "We'll cut through here and grab them."

The men began to chisel away at the ceiling. It crumbled easily, revealing the floor above. A trooper cut a shoulder width slit in the floor membrane and popped his head inside.

"It's an empty room," he said. "I'm going in."

He clambered through the gap and crouched silently on the floor. Another trooper followed him in. They were in a small windowless room with a door at one end. A small desk stood against a wall.

Two more troopers heaved themselves into the room, and the soldiers below passed them guns. The lead trooper signalled to move, and they walked softly, using the outside edges of their feet to cushion any sound, until they got to the door. He peered through a gap in the hinge – there was a corridor and a cell opposite. He could see a peep hole and an array of keys on a chain.

"We've come up in the wrong bloody room," he whispered.

Moving quickly, he grabbed the keys and tried the lock with the first one, no luck. The second slotted in perfectly. He twisted it and pushed the door open.

"Good morning, gentlemen," said Jameson, standing behind a bullet proof screen, and flanked by a dozen armed guards. "Good of you to drop by."

"It's a trap - abandon mission," shouted the trooper. The guards pounced, wrestling him to the ground. The others tried to help, but they were quickly pinned down.

"We never leave one behind," shouted Corporal Torrance, hearing the commotion. He scrambled into the dome, rushed into the cell and blasted two Space Corps guards before they could move.

Two more swivelled around to see him, and fired their blasters, missing him but striking their fellow men. In the mayhem, the troopers broke free and rushed out of the room. Corporal Torrance followed, giving covering fire. He blasted off one last round, then dived headfirst into the tunnel, landing on a pile of bodies.

"Let's get the hell out of here," he shouted, and they hobbled down the lava tube as fast as they could. When they got back to the sinkhole, they blew up the tunnel, causing its roof to collapse.

"Did you see the troopers?" asked Corporal Torrance.

"No, only Space Corps," said one of his men. "They were waiting for us."

Chapter 31: Debrief

"They must have had a tip off," said Captain Rossiter. "And it wasn't from one of my men."

"That's impossible," said Sally. "Only our most trusted were told about the mission."

"How else could they have known?" asked the captain.

"There is another possibility," said John. "It's just conceivable that they intercepted a radio transmission."

"All you need is a standard radio," I said, "I used to listen to the police on Earth that way."

"It's a possibility," said Sally. "One thing's for certain, they know about the extent of the lava tubes now."

"Who cares about the lava tubes when my men are locked up," said Captain Rossiter. "The explosion has blocked them with thousands of tons of rocks in any case. It would take months to dig it out."

Chapter 32: Truce

"Let's demand they hand over the prisoners or we blast our way in," I said, as we debated our next steps.

"Hold fire, soldier," said the captain. "Hot heads make bad decisions. Let's try every other avenue before we go nuclear."

"In any case, if the dome goes up, the troopers will go with them," said Sally. "John, what do you suggest?"

"You're not going to like it," he said, running a hand through his middle parting. "But the sensible way forward is to meet them half-way."

I felt my blood pressure rise but managed to keep my mouth shut for once.

"In what way, John?" asked Sally.

"We could say that we are prepared to go along with their suggestion that both sides down arms. But make it clear that the captain keeps a small armed police force. I can't see how they could argue with that."

"We could even offer to share power," said Sally. "Just so long as we make it clear that all the key jobs are held by Lots."

"Sounds like a plan," said the captain. "I can have something drawn up by sparrows'."

After the union rubber-stamped the proposals, they were sent to the Space Corps. We had learned our lesson, and there were no more face-to-face meetings. Instead, we did everything by mail, to prevent everyone getting hot headed.

The proposals went back and forth several times before a version was agreed 'in principle' and signed by both sides.

Within hours, the troopers were released and paraded around camp on the shoulders of their comrades. "It's a big first step. But let's keep our eyes on the prize – a peaceful resolution to the conflict," said Sally.

"But how are we supposed to stomach living with them after everything that's happened?" I asked.

"You won't have to socialise with them," she said. "We just have to live in peace."

It was gut wrenching.

A few days later, Commander Davey visited the sinkhole. She offered to send a team of experts to improve things at the farm. I kept my distance, remembering the prize.

But over the weeks and months, my mood gradually lifted. They helped us install an automated watering system, so the crop roots were never water-logged, or left too dry.

They also spotted a nutrient deficiency in the solution we were feeding the plants, so the crops grew stronger. And they helped us recalibrate the artificial lights to stop plants scorching.

Power sharing seemed to work okay too. They accepted a minority role, seemingly happy with the functions they controlled, such as energy and facilities. Each week a contingent of Space Corps moved in. And just six months after the documents were signed, most of them were living with us.

"It's almost as if nothing ever happened," I said to Sally as we mingled among them in camp.

Chapter 33: Commission

While Sally and I would have been happy to let life continue in this way for the sake of peace, our fellow Lots were not happy. To them, it looked as though the Space Corps had got away scot-free with mass murder. They lobbied the union, which demanded something be done to reconcile the past. The captain proposed a 'truth and reconciliation' commission, as an alternative to a criminal court. The union agreed.

"The commission is for restorative justice. It seeks reparations and forgiveness rather than retribution and punishment," said Sally, to everyone assembled in the hall for its inaugural meeting.

"We will be inviting victims of the Space Corps to give evidence about their experiences over the coming weeks," she added. "The perpetrators will be required to give testimony and request amnesty. We will create a register for those in the Space Corps who wish to express their regret."

"Objection," said Commander Davey. "All sides of the conflict should be included in the register. Both sides have committed crimes."

"Overruled," said Sally. "You cannot conflate the activities of the two sides. The Lots were always acting in self-defence."

We had the majority on Council, so there was nothing the commander could do about it.

"The commission will have the power to grant amnesty to those who committed abuses during the Space Corps era," Sally continued, reading from a script. "That is provided those abuses were proportionate and there is full disclosure by the person seeking amnesty."

I could see that Commander Davey was fuming. Her face had turned red, and her lips were pursed. "And what about those people who do not wish to take part?" she asked.

"They will face lengthy prison sentences," said Sally.

Three committees were set up. One for Human Rights led by Sally, a Reparations and Rehabilitation Committee led by Captain Rossiter and an Amnesty Committee, led by me.

It was all very ambitious considering the size of the colony, and our lack of legal training. But we had no choice given the mood of the Lots.

After a month, the commission had accounted for 12 murders under the Space Corps regime.

A total of 16 amnesty applications had been made, including by several members of the Space Corps' Council. But the slaughter of the troopers as they slept remained unresolved.

Commander Davey and Jameson were refusing to appear before the inquiry, calling it a "charade." They faced a sentence of up to two years, and being stripped of their places on the new unified council, unless they agreed.

Chapter 34: Double cross

It was a big day. Commander Davey had at last caved-in and was due in the dock. I was going to be called as a witness.

I typed up a story for Earth in my bungalow, before heading out for a walk to clear my mind:

Judgement day for Space Corps Commander.

As the truth and reconciliation commission continues its work on Mars, it has called on Commander Davey to give evidence about her role in crimes committed by the Space Corps.

I travelled with the commander to Mars and will be giving evidence against her today. High in my mind is the way she behaved on the flight from Earth....

As I walked through camp to the far side of the lake, I spotted a group of Space Corps officers chatting to some Lots. Laughter broke out. Perhaps we could make it work after all, I thought. Once the inquiry was over, we could move on to other things.

Sally was working on the colony's first five-year plan. With supplies from Earth dwindling, the colony would need to make a lot of things for itself.

Soap, paper and clothing were in short supply. A committee was tasked with filling the shortfalls. The spaceships would be stripped of everything. Nothing could be wasted. Some old skills would be needed too - cobblers, blacksmiths and tailors for starters.

There were no animals on Mars, other than a few insects that had snuck onboard the rockets, but we had a seedbank for four million plants. It would be my job to grow flax and other plants to provide raw materials for clothing.

My pager buzzed, giving notice that I was shortly to appear in front of the commission. I raced back to my digs and lay on my bed for a few minutes with my eyes shut, trying to recall everything that had happened to me since I'd set sail to Mars.

Hundreds of Lots were milling about the hall as I arrived. "Call next witness into Commander Davey's treatment of the people of Mars," said the commission's administrator.

"George Hodges, will you take your seat please."

I sat at the end of the table, with Sally facing me on the other side. Teams representing the Lots and Space Corps sat between us.

"When did you first meet Commander Davey?" asked Sally.

"During my first day of training on Earth," I said.

"And what was your impression of her?"

"She didn't seem to like the lottery winners," I said.

"How so?" asked Sally.

"It was clear that she resented us taking up places on Mars," I said.

"Objection, conjecture," said the Space Corps counsel.

"Overruled. We are trying to establish the witness's early impressions of Commander Davey," said the chair.

"Did your opinion change during the flight to Mars?"

"Not really, she remained unsympathetic. It was very much a case of 'them and us.'"

"And what was your reaction to that?"

"I was concerned," I said, glancing at the commander. She looked at the hall clock. It was nearly 2pm. "She had a poor grasp of reality in my view."

"Objection."

"Sustained," said the chair. "Let's not make it personal."

"Did she say anything else that concerned you?" asked Sally.

"She appeared to have a dystopian vision of how the colony should be run," I said. "Something along feudal lines."

Commander Davey took another look at the clock: 1:59pm and 35 seconds. She reached into her bag, pulled out a respirator and fixed it into position around her mouth. The rest of her team copied her. The air conditioning vents started to whirl. An emergency siren wailed out across the sinkhole.

"Gas attack," shouted Sally. "Make for the exits."

People started to panic, running in all directions. One toppled over. I grabbed her and raced to a door, Sally just behind me.

The exits were bolted but the troopers smashed them open with the heels of their boots, and I rushed outside with Sally.

"Get to the lava tube," she said.

A battle was raging around camp. The Space Corps were using butane gas bottles as flame throwers. Captain Rossiter and his troopers were firing back with plastic bullets. A large group of Lots were assembling at the entrance to the lava tube. Someone opened the door, and they poured inside.

I could see John standing with Commander Davey and Jameson across the lake. They were holding crossbows and fired a volley in our direction. A bolt whistled over our heads.

"Get inside," shouted Sally, and I followed her in. Captain Rossiter was the last through the door. He slammed it shut and slotted a bolt across the top to secure it.

"John is one of them," I said to Sally.

"I know, he'll have to go down with the others," she said.

"But they have the sinkhole," I said.

"We knew there was a mole," she said. "The only question was who?"

"You suspected him all along?"

"Only after the raid. That was unexplainable."

Captain Rossiter appeared at my shoulder.

"Everything is set," he said cooly.

"Then let's blow the sinkhole sky high," said Sally.

He flipped a switch and a dozen panels blew out of the dome's roof, sucking its atmosphere instantly into the void.

"It's over," said Sally.

"But how long can we last down here?" I asked.

"Long enough to rebuild the sinkhole," she said. "Then we can build a new colony free from the Space Corps."

About the author

Andrew Tristem is an author and journalist who has worked at many leading publications, including the Sunday Times, Sunday Express and Metro newspapers.

He started his career at the Western Gazette in Somerset before moving to the Hamstead & Highgate Express in London, where he ran one of the editions.

Andrew worked in government communications for 14 years, handling major events including the Fukushima nuclear disaster, COVID-19 pandemic and Ebola.

Andrew lives with his wife, Rebecca, and children, Toby and Rose, in Henley-on-Thames, near London. His first book, The Incidental Murderer, was published in 2016.